SOUND THE CHARGE

SOUND THE CHARGE

The Western Frontier: Spillman Creek to Summit Springs

by
Richard Weingardt

A JACQUELINE ENTERPRISES, INC. PUBLICATION
Englewood, Colorado 80110

ISBN 0-932446-00-0

MANUFACTURED IN THE UNITED STATES OF AMERICA
B & B Printers
104 F Street
Salida, CO 81201

Dedicated to
Nancy, Susan, David

SOUND THE CHARGE

TABLE OF CONTENTS

LIST OF ILLUSTRATIONS

BUFFALO BILL POSTER - BATTLE AT SUMMIT SPRINGS
Courtesy: Buffalo Bill Historical Center, Cody, Wyoming

Reenactment of the rescue at Summit Springs was the climax to many of the famous Buffalo Bill Wild West Shows. The poster displays the drama of the fight, which played to the crown heads of Europe as well as American audiences. The young, dashing Bill Cody was the chief of scouts for the U.S. 5th Cavalry at the battle.

INTRODUCTION

In the summer of 1869, the U. S. 5th Cavalry and the Southern Cheyenne Dog Soldiers engaged in the greatest Indian battle fought on the Colorado high plains. Summit Springs was possibly the most important battle on the entire Central Plains, and one of the notable conflicts between the whiteman and the Indian on the American frontier. Led by General Carr, with Buffalo Bill as his Chief of Scouts, twice as many soldiers as were at Custer's last stand participated. It lacks the controversy of Sand Creek, which really was a massacre, and ranks with the Beecher Island battle for endurance and heroics by soldiers. At Sand Creek a little over 100 Indian lodges were in camp, while the Summit Springs village contained 84.

The saga began with the capture of white women at Spillman Creek, Kansas, and included a relentless chase by the Army out of Fort McPherson, Nebraska. The battle provided a spine chilling Cavalry charge and a daring rescue of hostages. Tall Bull, the famous Dog Soldier leader, defended his people with suicidal valor. It was the last engagement with the Plains Indians in Colorado and opened the territory to the western migration. It allowed the completion of the Central Kansas Railroad to Denver in 1870.

This is one of the true, colorful stories of the western frontier, of the hardy pioneers, and of the dismal relationship developed between the whiteman and American Indian. The Indian, who desired above all to continue his way of life, was deprived of his hunting grounds, was defeated in battle, and was pressured to settle down. He experienced the carnage of the buffalo, indispensable for food and housing, the rapid firing guns, and the spread of whiteman's diseases. All were lethal to him.

The whiteman experienced the Indian's wrath. About white women, Colonel Richard Irving Dodge, in *The Plains of the Great West,* is poignantly descriptive.

"I believe I am perfectly safe in the assertion that there is not a single wild tribe of Indians in all the wide territory of the United States which does not regard the person of the female captive as the inherent right of the captor, and I venture to assert further that in the last twenty-five years no woman has been taken prisoner by any plains Indians who did not as soon after as practicable become a victim to the lust of every one of her captors....

No words can express the horror of the situation of that most unhappy woman who falls into the hands of these savage fiends. The husband or other male protectors killed or dispersed, she is borne off in triumph to where the Indians make their first camp. Here, if she makes no resistance, she is laid upon a buffalo robe, and each in turn violates her person, the others dancing, singing, and yelling around her. If she resists at all, her clothing is torn off from her person, four pegs are driven into the ground, and her arms and legs, stretched to the utmost, are tied fast to them by thongs. Here, with the howling band dancing and singing around her, she is subjected to violation after violation, outrage after outrage, to every abuse and indignity, until not unfrequently death releases her from suffering. The Indian woman, knowing this inevitable consequence of capture, makes no resistance, and gets off comparatively easy. The white woman naturally and instinctively resists, is 'staked out,' and subjected to the fury of passions fourfold increased by the fact of her being white and a novelty....

The Indians prefer, if possible, to take female captives, white women especially, one moderately good looking being worth as many ponies as would buy three or four Indian girls. Besides this, they are exceedingly valuable when the tribe gets tired of the

> war path and intimates its desire for peace with the United States. The Indians take great credit to themselves for bringing in these captives, invariably demanding a large price; while the Government, as eager for peace as a schoolboy after a thrashing, instead of punishing the villians for their outrages, pats them on the back, and tells them that they are good fellows for bringing in the prisoners, and pays the price demanded."

In 1869, the Civil War was over. Grant was President, and there was a flood of immigrants to the West. Settlers came with only the clothes on their backs, their bare hands, and knowledge of their trade, which was not necessarily farming. For men the West offered a possible new life, wealth, excitement and freedom; it offered women fear from the violence and wildness surrounding them. Most travel was by horse, wagon or stage coach. The railroad was just beginning to operate on the western frontier. The electric light by Edison was not perfected until 1879. The Bell telephone was not invented until 1876.

Primary sources, including Carr's official report and reminiscenses used for most publications on Summit Springs and Spillman Creek, are included in Part Two of this book for serious history students. First-hand material from their experiences with the Cheyenne by both George Grinnel, and George Hyde is also included. These eyewitness accounts are extremely entertaining, showing that reading truth can be as exciting as fiction.

Though a full text has never been assembled on the Summit Springs story, articles have been published. A thorough documentary, to a large extent based on official correspondence between Carr and his superiors, has been compiled by Dr. James P. King on both the Republican River Expedition and the Battle. The conflict between Luther North, on his brother's behalf, and Buffalo Bill about Chief Tall Bull is extensively reviewed by Don Russel in *The Lives and Legends of*

Buffalo Bill. Interviews with settlers at Spillman Creek are the background for histories by Barr, Bernhardt, and Roenigk on Lincoln County, Kansas.

The Narrative, Part One, is intended as a reading history not a historical documentary. For those unfamiliar with the whiteman and the Southern Cheyenne Indian encounters, The Chronology, Part Three, is recommended reading prior to starting The Narrative. Maps are also furnished in Chapter Ten.

The following are acknowledged for their helpful assistance: Nancy Sherbert, Margaret Briggs, and Terry Harmon, Kansas State Historical Society; Judy Golden, The State Historical Society of Colorado; Duane Miles, Sterling Journal-Advocate; Ann Reinert and Don Snoddy, Nebraska State Historical Society; Pam Rose, Denver Public Library, Western History Department; Mildred Elliott, Logan County Historical Society; Peter Hassrick and Sheri Hoem, Buffalo Bill Historical Center; Kathy Wacker, Julesburg Advocate; Betty Ebke, Sedgwick County Historical Society; James and Loa Page, Lincoln County Historical Society; Stewart Butler, Navy and Old Army Branch, National Archives; Dorothy Richards, Hays Public Library, Kansas Room; A. Virgil Christiansen; Ruth Dunn; Timothy Kloberdanz; Patricia Shroeder; Marguerite Strange; Garey Dickinson for the maps; and above all others to my wife, Evie, who not only shared in gathering material and research for this book but has, also, given understanding and encouragement.

PART I

AN INDIAN WAR PARTY
(Oil by W. C. Wyeth)
Courtesy: Northern National Gas Company Collection, Joslyn Art Museum Omaha, Nebraska

CHAPTER 1

PROLOGUE

In the latter part of the nineteenth century, America witnessed a large influx of foreigners. Europe was suffering from the natural misfortunes of drought and famine, and was in a climate of economic, political and social unrest. Many were ready to leave their fatherland for the American frontier, a land of opportunity and adventure.

The Homestead Act encouraged these new immigrants to move West. It only took fencing off half an acre of sod and filing a notice of intent to claim a quarter section of one hundred and sixty acres as your own land, your new home. The price was $1.25 an acre. But it was money that could go for months or years without being paid, since the land could not be sold until the government surveys were completed.

New settlers, immigrants, still speaking their foreign languages, made their way to this open land. Among these pioneers were George Weichell and his beautiful, young wife, Maria. Arriving in New York on a cold day in February, they reached Lincoln County, Kansas by train in early April, 1869. Germans from Hanover, George was a brewer about thirty years old; Maria was twenty and refined. He spoke some English, and she, none at all. To the other settlers it was evident they were educated people, and their clothing and material possessions reflected their wealthy background. With them came a family employee, Fred Meigerhoff. He had served them as a gardener in the old country, but he would equal them as their neighbor in the new land.

Ferdinand Erhardt, with whom they stayed for a short time, showed the men a claim near his on Bullfoot Creek. He was a seasoned frontiersman, knew George Custer, Wild Bill Hickock, Buffalo Bill Cody, and had fought Indians. They considered his advice, but while they were at the local Schermerhorn ranch and general store, they met several of the Danish settlers from Spillman Creek. These men spoke a common language and convinced Weichell and Meigerhoff the area surrounding their settlement a short distance away was more fertile.

Though Erhardt warned the Germans that Indians had previously terrorized the Spillman Creek area, and would probably do so again, the newcomers made the trip to Junction City, Kansas, to file their claims for land along the Spillman. At this same time, May 10, they also filed their citizenship papers. They would learn Erhardt's advice on Indians was sound.

In the spring, 1869, the Civil War was over, and American democracy had stood the blow of its first Presidential assassination. The developing railroads promised to make all of America a land without frontiers. With tracks spanning the continent, Union Pacific and Central Pacific Railroads met at Promontory Point, Utah, where Leland Stanford, President of Central Pacific and Thomas Durant, Vice-President of Union Pacific, drove the final gold spike, opening the transcontinental rail system. Civilization was coming to the West. But almost a century after the United States declared itself a nation, and shortly after the freedom for Negros, it was still fighting an internal struggle with the natives of America, the Indian nations.

Although Custer's massacre of Black Kettle's village had been reported as the final victory over the Southern Cheyenne Indian rebellion, it had actually kindled the renegade faction. General Sheridan and army officials would soon find that it would take more than a single raid to defeat the fierce Dog Soldier warriors.

Little Robe, now the leading chief of the tribe with Black Kettle dead, was determined to lead his people back to the reservation where they might at least live in peace. He wanted to settle down at Camp Supply with Little Raven and his Arapahoe tribe. The Dog Soldiers opposed him. Their famous commander, Tall Bull, accused Little Robe of being just like Black Kettle and of only serving the whiteman's purposes. He declared the Cheyenne warriors would never make a peace that compelled them to settle on a reservation. The Cheyenne had always been a free people, and they would remain free or die. It would take all his valor and brilliance to back up this boast.

In turn Little Robe blamed the Dog Soldiers for making trouble with the army. Every time they went out on a war party, the whole tribe suffered. The renegades were a threat to their own people. When they refused to sacrifice their warrior activities for Little Robe's peaceful resolve, he banished them from the reservation. He also threatened to join the whites and drive them out if they would not go willingly. The split was irreversible.

Tall Bull and White Horse with one hundred sixty-five lodges of Dog Soldiers, two hundred warriors and their families, started north to join the Northern Cheyenne and Red Cloud's Sioux in Wyoming, Montana and the Black Hills. They stopped off to pick up the band who had stayed the winter on the Republican River. They were also joined by a few Arapahoe and bands of Sioux, under the leadership of Whistler and Pawnee Killer. While they were camped at Beaver Creek making ready for the long march, suddenly, one day in early May, 1869, without warning, the U. S. Fifth Cavalry charged. The Dog Soliders fought hard to save their women and children. Most managed to escape, but twenty-five Indians died in battle. For the survivors, it was a bitter memory.

The charge had been led by the enthusiastic Civil War hero, bearded General E. Carr. He was thirty-nine, young enough to feel disappointed with such minor victories, but not discouraged. With no further thought concerning the repercussions of his actions, he led his Fifth Cavalry to their new assignment at Fort McPherson, Nebraska. Their transfer was being made from Fort Lyons, Colorado.

After this, Tall Bull's bands began ferocious raids on frontier settlements and homesteads in western Kansas. On May 21, thirty to forty warriors armed with guns, spears, bows and arrows surprised a four man buffalo hunting party. When their ammunition gave out, the Indians annihilated them.

They did not neglect the hated railroad. One week later, two miles of the Kansas Pacific track at Fossil Creek Station was ripped out and the railroad crew attacked. Killed were John Lynch and Alexander McKeefer, a Canadian and a giant of a man. George Taylor, George Seely, Charley Sylvester, and Adolph Roenigk were wounded but lived to talk about it.

The Dog Soldiers then headed for the homesteads on Spillman Creek and the bloody Memorial Day Massacre.

INDIAN ATTACK AT FOSSIL STATION
The sketch of the Cheyenne Dog Soldiers ripping up the hated railroad cutting through their hunting grounds was given to Lincoln County, Kansas, by Historian Adolph Roenigk.

CHAPTER 2

CAPTURE

A lone horseman was first sighted, riding fast to the west. He would appear on the hills and disappear, then reappear. John Alverson did not like the mystery. Then they all appeared. They rode as soldiers, keeping four abreast as they crossed the hills in the blue distance. On first watching them, nineteen year old, Eli Zeigler, who was with John Alverson, was curious but without apprehension. Though small, their settlement along Spillman Creek was developing rapidly, and he thought it not unusual that the army should show a protective interest. He was sure they were soldiers riding to the Solomon.

But as the horsemen rode towards the men in the wagon with increasing speed, the two friends saw the Indians for what they were. At the first rifle shots, the two men jumped from their wagon and ran for the heavily wooded stream. They could still hear them firing, as they worked their way down to a narrow hiding place where the banks rose high. The Indians soon gave up their search and rode onward. But the young men were experienced frontiersmen and wary of Indian ways. Both had been at Beecher Island, the Mulberry Scrape, and other Indian fights. They remained hidden.

They would later learn that these Indians were the feared Cheyenne Dog Soldiers, renegades, who had refused the reservation peace. Their leader had declared that they would die for their land and their freedom. If they were to die, they would die in battle, with whitemen dying all around. In the short time the men of this Indian war society had the horse, they had become the finest horsemen in the world. They were superior to the average Army trooper in shooting at a gallop. Their tactics included ambush, strike and retreat.

Zeigler and Alverson resolved to stay in hiding until nightfall when they might return to the settlement in safety. There were others that bloody day who were not so lucky.

It was a Sunday, Memorial Day 1869, a day for visiting and enjoying the innocent pleasures of settlement life. Having finished their noon meal, Eskild Lauritzen and his wife Stine started for the neighboring Christiansen farm. For a time their son walked with them, but he was not so interested in the beauties of nature, as impatient to play with the youngest Christiansen boy. When his parents lingered to compare their new crops with those they had harvested in Denmark*, he went on without them. Left to themselves, the couple enjoyed the spring sunshine. The tall prairie grass bent like waves to the wind, while the treeless horizon of low rolling hills held back a clear expanse of sky. They had a small log cabin on their claim which they shared with the Weichell couple, Meigherhoff, and Petersen, seven people. The others were over at their claims spending time much the same as they were now doing.

Suddenly war whoops startled the Lauritzens. They were completely surprised. Their murdered bodies were left lying side by side. She had been viciously disrobed, only her stockings and dress hoops were left on her bloody body.

Otto Petersen was staking out his garden close by when the first war cry rang out. With only a hatchet to defend himself, he was soon scalped and mutilated with his own weapon. As a jeweler, the young man was a worthy victim. The Indians carried off his trinkets and jewelry in high triumph. He was from the same area of Denmark as the Lauritzens and had

* Haderslev, Northern Germany, the area ceded from Denmark to Germany in 1865. The Christiansens, Lauritzens, and Petersen had all arrived in Kansas during February, 1869.

immigrated to avoid the army draft in Germany. He did not avoid the noble native, the American redman.

As the Indians advanced, the Christiansen family took shelter in the dugout they had built into the Spillman Creek river bank. The Lauritzen boy was already with them. Though he dreaded the fate of his parents, he was grateful to be behind stone walls with ready ammunition to keep the Indians at bay. The Indians repeatedly tried to set fire to the house, but the Christiansen brothers, blacksmiths from Denmark, had built well and fought bravely. Realizing their actions were unprofitable, the renegades left in search of easier prey.

They didn't have far to look. That afternoon George and Maria Weichell along with their family friend and employee, Fred Meigherhoff, were inspecting their newly filed claim. Between the three of them, they agreed it was the finest farmland in Lincoln County; it would make the beginnings of their farming empire. George had always found himself among men admiring his attractive wife, and now he was proud of his new land. Besides this, he had money, even though there were few things to buy in frontier Kansas, he felt himself content and better off than most.

Maria had particular reason to be happy that day. Though she could not yet speak the language of this new land, it seemed to hold the promise of a bright future for her. She was young, married to a rich and handsome man who had taken her from the boredom of the Prussian drawing rooms to this American adventure. Kansas in many ways was like her Germany, with beautiful, green grass valleys; only without trees and wilder. She had even seen her first American buffalo on her trip West. When George had returned from Junction City, after filing for their land, she ran to him and cuddled in his arms. She now had reason to believe she was carrying his child; the first of many children, she hoped. She dreamt about their new life in this new land.

Gunfire and shouts broke her reverie. The immigrants had nowhere to hide. Maria's bright silk dress and glittering jewelry flashed in the sun. Protectively, the men drew close around her. They fought their way down the valley, keeping the Indians off with their guns. But a mile and a half west of Lincoln Center, their ammunition gave out.

As the men were killed and scalped, Maria struggled against a warrior's hold. But when she saw them cut off her husband's fingers for his rings, her eyes glazed over with shock.

Sounds of the Indian attack carried to a Sunday gathering at the home of Nicholas Whalen. At these first signs of trouble, Thomas Noon and his wife saddled their horses and fled. Whalen left Mrs. Susanna Alderdice and Mrs. Timothy Kine in his house alone with their small children, unprotected and unmounted, so that he might corral his horses in a safer place.

Thinking their only hope was to hide by the river, the women started for it, each carrying their youngest child. Susanna's three sons, aged seven, four and a half, and two years old, kept what pace they could. With the small children and Susanna's third month of pregnancy, their gait was no faster than a walk.

When they saw warriors riding towards them at full gallop, Mrs. Kine ran for the river. Susanna begged her to stay, but Mrs. Kine's first thought was for the safety of her child. Holding the baby high, she rushed into the water. It was deep enough to cover her shoulders, but she crossed safely, and hid with her child in the lay of a fallen tree.

Overcome with fear, Susanna collapsed on the ground. The Indians immediately shot her three sons, but when she pleaded for the life of her infant daughter, the baby was spared. The bodies of the boys were left punctured with arrows.

As the Indians searched for Mrs. Kine, they passed so near she could have touched them. But her hiding place was well chosen and her baby girl kept silent, unaware of the danger. Their moccasins didn't make much noise. Each time their fringed leather leggings would pass by her, it was even hard for her to breathe. After some time the Indians rode on, taking Susanna and her baby captive. Mrs. Kine and her baby daughter (who later married John Linker) fled to Fred Erhardt's house late in the night; wet, cold, and thoroughly frightened.

That same evening, 14-year old Harrison Strange and Arthur Schmutz were digging turnips on a hill overlooking Lincoln Center and the Saline River when they saw two Indians riding towards them. The boys started to run, but the older Indian indicated they were friendly. The boys waited to see what they wanted. The middle-aged Indian rode up and tapped each of the boys with his spear, counting coup. Then he galloped after some loose horses while the teenaged Indian approached the boys. When he was very close, he raised himself high and with a wood club in both hands struck Strange, smashing his skull. Discarding his club, the youth shot the fleeing Schmutz with an arrow. By force of will, the boy continued to run and dodge until the older Strange brothers saw his trouble and chased the Indian off. They were the sons of Reverend Strange, 38, a native of Indiana who had been in Lincoln County since 1866.

Early the next day the Lauritzen boy and the Christiansens; Lorentz, his wife and baby girl, and Peder, his wife and three children, Helena, Christian, Hans, hurried to the local gathering place, Lon Schermerhorn's ranch on Elkhorn Creek.

Later that day, the settlers* gathered their dead. When they found the bodies of Weichell and Meigherhoff, they feared for Maria's safety. The only sign of her were her delicate footprints, almost lost in the trampling of horses.

They buried Petersen, Stine and Eskild Lauritzen along Spillman Creek where the found them.**

---

* Settlers aiding included: J. J. (Jack) Peate, Volney Ball, Ed Johnson, Isaac Degraff, D. C. Skinner, Richard Clark, who became first sheriff of Lincoln County, William Thompson, George Green, Chal Smith, Z. Ivy, Charles Martin, A. Campbell, Aaron Bell, Polk Tripp, Fletcher Vilott, Hutchinson Farley, whose father was killed at Beecher's Island, Thomas Boyle, John Lyden, and John Haley.

** The Strange boy was buried on the Schermerhorn Ranch (later moved to Lincoln Cemetery) and the Alderdice children on their Grandfather Zeigler's farm.

Arthur Schmutz was taken to Fort Harker, Kansas, suffered in the hospital there for 10 weeks and died in August. He was thirteen years old.

At the scene of Susanna's abduction, they found one of her sons, four and one-half year old Willis Daily, still alive. They carried him to the house of Martin (Uncle Mart) Hendrickson, where Phil Lance and Washington Smith removed the arrow with a large pair of bullet molds. There Tom Alderdice heard his young stepson's version of his wife's capture.

Alderdice, John Strange, Mart Hendrickson and a few other neighbors had gone to Salina, Kansas on May 30th for supplies and other business. The next day when they heard Indians were on the warpath, they raced their horses back to Lincoln Center. The men were no strangers to Indian warfare. Hendrickson, a man of unusual strength, had only last year aided a nude, tortured Mrs. Janie Bacon in her escape from the Indians. Alderdice, a rugged frontiersman, was one of the heroic Forsyth Scouts at the Beecher Island Battle. He didn't know, however, when he left his wife Sunday morning, that he would never see Susanna again.

THE CAPTIVE
(Oil by Eugene Shortridge)
Courtesy: Western Publications, Inc. Austin, Texas.

CHAPTER 3

THE CHASE

The Indians disappeared as suddenly as they had come. The night of the raid they camped near the Bullfoot Creek cave, but the next morning they were gone. It was then that Susanna became aware her captors had another white woman: the wealthy, young Prussian woman, the one with all the silk dresses. They were of different cultures, could not speak each other's language, but were to share a strange, painful existence together.

A few days after their attack on Spillman Creek, the Indians heading northwest attacked a party of four buffalo hunters: Solomon Humbarger, Dick Alley, William Earl, and Harry Trask. From there they again broke into small bands harrassing settlers, and attacking and derailing the Kansas Pacific Railroad at Grinnell. Each atrocity brought public outcry as the newspapers demanded protection from the Indians. Something had to be done.

The U. S. Army was in an embarrassing position. Earlier Custer had sent one hundred men of the 7th Cavalry from Ft. Hays, Kansas, to find the hostiles. But along the Solomon River none had been found, nor was it known the exact identity of the Indian raiders. Still, their presence in Republican River country remained painfully evident.

General Carr's face must have hardened as he read his orders from General Christopher Auger. He had just returned to Fort McPherson for a brief reorganization, and now only two weeks later, his orders were to drive the renegade Indians from the Republican River country. It was not the fatigue, nor the danger that he minded. He had come out West as an Indian fighter by way of West Point then the Civil War. He well knew the hardships of a soldier's life. His instructions read, "The object of your expedition is to drive the Indians out of Republican Country and to follow them as far as possible. Most of the details of the operation must be left to your judgment." The details, it seemed to Carr, must be left largely to luck and the elusiveness of the Indians. He was prepared to fight the Indians and drive them wherever they might best be driven. How he was to go about finding them in the first place, then catching them, was the problem.

The bearded war eagle would be taking on the wiley, forty-year old master of Plains Indian guerrilla warfare, Chief Tall Bull. The most noted and most feared Dog Soldier warrior of all. He was tall, lithe and proud, his people's last hope for freedom. He would be as cunning and intelligent an adversary as any Carr had met. His famed bands were completely at home on the prairies and sandhills. Their lookouts were posted at high points where warning smoke signals could be seen for long distances. When they were discovered, they would break trail. Choosing places where hoof prints could not be detected easily, they would turn off, a few at a time, until there was no trail to follow. If lack of time prohibited such subtlety, they would simply disperse, leaving so many trails it was impossible to follow. Afterwards they would meet at some designated place and resume their hostile activities or camp.

Carr's command would consist of ten companies of the Fifth Cavalry, supplemented by Pawnee scouts. Two companies would remain at Fort McPherson, while eight would take to the field. It seemed like a small force to be sent into the heart of hostile Indian country. Not only this, but the rugged land the Army had to face would take its toll. This was to be Carr's first use of the Pawnee. He was apprehensive, though their white commander, Major Frank North, would prove he could keep them under control. The Pawnee called North, *Pa-nile-*

shar, (Chief of the Pawnee) which was a title of respect they had given only one other white man, John Fremont.

Whatever his feeling about the Pawnee, Carr had no doubt about the cavalry's Chief of Scouts, "Buffalo Bill" Cody. Cody, the buffalo hunter, had shown skill and bravery as a Pony Express rider at the age of fourteen. During the years 1867-1868, he killed 4,280 buffalo supplying the railroad meat. His nickname spoke for his reputation as a true plainsman and good rifle shot. Carr had worked with Cody in the winter campaign of 1868, and specifically requested that the twenty-three year old be retained as Chief of Scouts for the Republican River Country expedition.

His officers were all experienced and equal to the task ahead. Second and third in command were Major (Brevet Colonel) William Bedford Royall and Major Eugene Wilkinson Crittenden. Royall was a hero of the Civil War and Crittenden was the nephew of Senator John J. Crittenden of Kentucky. Four troop commanders in the campaign were Captains George Price, Maley Cushing, Samuel Sumner, son of "Bull" Sumner, and Lester Walker. Young William Volkman would be the topographical officer to update maps of the wild land.

Now it only remained for Carr to lead his troops into open country, down Medicine Creek to the Republican River valley in the hopes that they might trail and encounter the renegade Indians. On June 9, 1869, after a full dress review, General Carr led the Fifth Cavalry out of Fort McPherson, Nebraska. With flags flying and bands playing, the three hundred mile expedition had begun. That night two terrified young women huddled, soaked from a torrential thunderstorm, fearful of their future, unaware that a rescue party was in pursuit.

The rescuers began slowly. Pulling the wagons through the sand hills of the Platte River Valley, the Army mules tired quickly. The ground shifted beneath them, and many of their loads overturned. The procession traveled only a few miles the first few days.

Troop morale depreciated when one of the captains exhibited

suicidal tendencies. On the third day, Carr called the command to a halt, ordering it to camp while he cared for Captain J. C. Denny, one of his veteran officers. Realizing that the Captain's grief over the recent death of his wife had left him unfit to command the troops, Carr ordered an escort of troopers to guard the officer back to Fort McPherson where he was placed in the post hospital. The next day he put a revolver to his head and killed himself. Under the shadow of this distressing news, Carr ordered his troops onward.

In the meantime, news had reached them of Indian raids in the lower Solomon settlements of Ottawa county. The hostiles had made scattered attacks, killing farmers, stealing stock, plundering and burning farms. Advancing in this direction, the Cavalry sighted a band of twenty warriors. The Indians dashed over the hill and were gone. Carr sent a company with some Pawnee to follow the trail. But the pursuit party soon discovered the trail scattered in different directions. The trail was lost.

For the next three days the soldiers marched on through the Republican River Valley. No Indians had been seen since their first encounter on June 12 but it was certain that the Indians were somewhere in the area. About mid-day on June 15, the expedition halted and camped on the banks of the Republican River. Shortly after, there were war whoops and a teamster galloped into camp with an arrow sticking in his back. He had been wounded when attackers tried to drive off the command's mules.

Cody, Royall and North led several companies in a running fight with the hostiles. Although the chase lasted until nightfall, only two of the marauders were killed. After losing the war party's trail, the soldiers returned to their moonlit camp.

At daylight, the command took up the trail. It was clearly marked and soon became heavy enough to indicate a large Indian party. When the trail crossed the swollen waters of Prairie Dog Creek, the troops left their supply wagons and followed the Indians' path south for another twenty-five miles.

Near the Solomon River their tracks again scattered in all directions. The trail was lost once more.

However, unknown to the soldiers, the main Indian village was moving swiftly west, up the Republican. Again it seemed that there was not an army in the West that could catch a fleeing Indian tribe.

When their captors stopped without warning, made camp, smeared on new war paint, and started chanting, dancing and waving scalps, Maria was confused. Susanna was not. She was fearful. She was a frontier woman and knew Indian ways. The warriors were making ready for their grand entrance into a main Indian village. Both women would be displayed, offered as trophies and exposed to a new wave of abuse.

After the victory celebration upon joining the village, Maria was taken to a chief's lodge. His war exploits were painted on the "dew cloth" lining. Susanna was taken to a different lodge alone. Her baby had long since been taken by her captors.

And suddenly there he was, Tall Bull himself emerging through the crowd, large, dark and foreboding. His patronage would free Maria from the abuse of the young braves, but would subject her to the wrath of his jealous women.

On June 17, after being deluged by a torrential rainstorm, Major Frank North and a newly recruited company of Pawnee joined the command. At the same time, Carr was delivered orders to detach Captain Sweatman's company for the protection of the Little Blue settlements. In exchange, Carr was given another fifty untried Pawnee scouts. This was an inconvenience as well as a dangerous risk. It was taken as a sign of indifference by the Fifth Cavalry's superiors and the public.

This further aggravated the General, who felt that the hardships of the Regiment were not fully appreciated since there had been no brilliant victories or even large scale battles. In the aftermath of the Civil War, the public looked on Indian fighting as one of the Army's unpleasant but necessary duties. Though the cavalry was the pride of the Army against fighting Indians, duty in the West many times offered little opportunity for either glamour or heroism.

The frustrated Army spent the next ten days wandering through the rolling hills of the Republican Valley. The swift Indians outdistanced them and stayed in hiding. The rugged country made the going rough for the wagons. There continued to be a shortage of supplies. The necessity of finding water for themselves and their animals restricted the Army's movements. Disease spread among the soldiers and two ambulances overflowed with the sick.

Conditions were monotonous from day to day. The soldiers would break camp, scout, travel and set up camp again. Night sleep was many times broken by yipping coyotes and restless horses. For diversion and supplementary rations they hunted buffalo. An occasional bucking bronco offered entertainment.

Also, Carr had brought along his greyhounds which he bragged could catch anything. The first time antelope were encountered he turned them loose to chase. Almost immediately the dogs were outdistanced by the fleet "plains deer" which caused Cody to remark to the General that, if anything, the antelope were a little ahead. Everyone but Carr laughed. Eventually he grinned and agreed, but kept the dogs under wraps from then on, except to catch jack rabbits, which they did easily.

A few days after the Dog Soldiers' attempted mule raid, the Pawnee scouts surrounded a small buffalo herd and killed thirty-two.

Cody, tall, lean and clad in fringed buckskins, his long wavy, brown hair flowing, flamboyantly made his presence known. Amused, the buffalo hunter wanted to show the Indians how to kill buffalo. Everyone agreed. Riding his favorite mount, Buckskin Joe, he shot thirty-six buffalo in a half mile run, almost one per shot and equally spaced fifty feet apart. The Pawnee were more than impressed with what they had witnessed.

When the Dog Soldiers would be sighted again, it would be Independence Day, with the rest of the nation celebrating.

During the unproductive period until then, the command moved steadily westward. Timber grew sparse. Away from the river valley, the hills were now covered with cactus, sage brush and buffalo grass. There was little camouflage for either the Indians or the Army. Late in June, Company "B", 9th Infantry, commanded by Captain Owen with twenty-six men arrived at Fort Sedgwick from San Francisco. Men in the frontier fort in northeast Colorado were not aware that Carr was chasing hostile Indians toward them.

On the afternoon of July 3, the Fifth Cavalry's time of waiting was at an end. A scouting party brought Carr news of an Indian camp less than thirty-six hours old. Thirty lodges had been in camp; not a hunting party, but part of Tall Bull's main village. Numerous mule shoes were found. There had been female shoe prints found too; signs that the women prisoners were still alive.

With this news, the pursuit took on new urgency. Carr knew the probable sufferings of women prisoners. Rather than accept capture, many frontiersmen saved their last bullet for themselves. Women were normally forced to become tribal slaves; to be starved, beaten and abused by the squaws, as well as being violated by the braves. To steal a woman was correlated with counting coup. Women were not only property, but also were conceptualized as the enemy. It was also known that polygamy was acceptable to any Indian man whose desire was not satisfied by a single spouse. It only mattered that he could support his women.

Leading a detachment of three companies along with fifty Pawnee scouts, Major Royall tracked the hostiles. Their trail led up the North Fork (Arickaree) of the Republican. But the Indians were moving cautiously. They scattered on leaving camp and drove their animals in every direction to confuse the trail.

After three days, Royall's patrol sighted a war party of twelve hostiles carrying a wounded warrior, Howling Magpie, on a litter. The excited Pawnee started in pursuit and the troops had no choice but to follow. The small group of Dog Soldiers was no match for Royall's detachment. They took three enemy scalps and captured eight horses. Nine warriors escaped.

The chase had circled back almost to its original starting point so Royall's patrol rejoined the main command. When Carr was informed of the skirmish, he was frustrated. The Pawnee had a victory scalp dance that night to celebrate their success, which Carr could only view as a blunder. Now the main Indian village would be alerted.

On July 8th, the Fifth Cavalry turned back down the river; it looked to the hostile Indians like a retreat. Three men from Company "M" were bringing in a stray horse several miles to the rear of the main column when eight Indians attacked. Corporal John Kyle led the others to a large rock which they used for a breast work on one side, while they killed the horse for defense on the other. From this position, they beat off the Indians, wounding two badly. In recognition for his special bravery in this encounter, Kyle would later receive the Congressional Medal of Honor.

Though the hostiles' main force was yet to be found, the retreating soldiers were close enough to make the Indians uneasy. At midnight the same day, five Dog Soldiers charged among the horses, yelling and firing into the camp. Mad Bear, the Sergeant of the Pawnee guard, ran after one of the Indians whose horse had fallen.

Just as he was about to overtake him, he was shot down by a cavalry bullet. The soldiers did a lot of shooting, but fired wildly. Though none of the marauders were hurt, they failed in their attempt to stampede the horses. Mad Bear's minor wounds were the only serious consequence of the night raid.

On the following day Carr, without fanfare, abruptly turned and headed north. Their exhausting march took them from the Arickaree toward the Frenchman Creek. After thirty miles without water, they camped.

The Pawnee came upon two old men and a woman following the main Dog Soldier village. They killed them.

The command then continued its forced march through the sandhills. It was hot and dry. The sun beat down relentlessly during the sixty-five mile march. They turned west upon reaching the Frenchman fork and crossed the winding stream several times. The dusty, tired soldiers passed two Indian camps, and by the end of July 10th stopped at the third, less than twenty-four hours old. In one day they had covered the territory the Indians had traveled in three. Women's shoe prints were found at each camp. All out pursuit was without question.

Realizing the Indians were about a day's march away, Carr selected only those men whose horses were still fit for service to make the final onslaught. The heavy wagon train would be left behind under guard of those unable to make the march. The column would march at daybreak. He had begun the expedition with eight companies of the Fifth Cavalry, almost five hundred soldiers. But now, at this critical time, he had available for service only two hundred and forty-four soldiers and fifty Pawnee scouts. There was no way of knowing the number of Dog Soldiers in the renegade camp. Unknown to the Army the Indian village was now only twenty miles northwest of them.

Tomorrow the two adversaries would surely meet in battle: Carr, dogged and determined; Tall Bull, cunning, elusive, but unsuspecting.

As tensions mounted, perceptions became distorted. "Indian fever" was in the air. Twice the morning of July eleventh Indians had been sighted, only to be confirmed as wild horses or bushes at closer range. But the soldiers were taking no chances. When they did, in fact, see two distant horsemen, the whole command reined up in a ravine until the warriors were out of sight.

At one point, the Indian trail divided. One side was plainly marked, while the other was dim. Carr assumed that the renegades expected him to follow the defined trail. Guessing they needed water as much as his men, Carr gambled and took the fainter trail towards Valley Station on the Platte.

As they were nearing the Platte River, scouts reported a herd of animals to the right. Others told of Indians seen on the table land to the left. Colonel Royall took Cody and three companies in search of the animals, while Carr led the rest of the command toward the Indian sighting, which was in the direction of the main trail. Both parties struck out on a gallop. Within minutes, Carr received the report that "teepees" had been sighted ahead. He sent to Colonel Royall for an extra company. Royall immediately returned his strongest unit with the Chief of Scouts leading it.

But as Carr rode on, there was no immediate sign of Indians. For an hour he led his men through the low hills of loose sand. It was after two p.m. The animals had not had water since morning, and they suffered from the hard painstaking pace they had traveled.

Colonel Royall returned to the command. He had traveled twenty miles in finding the reported animals were only bushes. Again, it seemed their expectations were defeated. The chase would continue across the Platte and past the railroad to the north. The Dog Soldiers would escape.

Still the disheartened Cavalry pushed onward until, at last, a herd of animals was sighted about four miles off in the hills. Having been so often disappointed, Carr assumed they were buffalo but decided to continue in that direction.

The Pawnee seemed certain of what lay ahead. They began to strip themselves for action, leaving only enough of their uniforms to identify themselves from the hostile Indians. They discarded their saddles at the same time. The Cavalry also prepared, making ready their gear. They quieted their sweating mounts and steadied their nerves. The only sounds were creaking saddles, and the occasional clinking of sabers or spurs.

Their preparations made, the men spurred their mounts and the column pressed onward. Keeping well hidden in the depressions between the sand hills, they moved rapidly to a deep valley northwest of the place assumed to contain the Indian camp. Within about a mile of this location, upon nearing the peak of the hill between the valleys, finally, the Indians were sighted. In the Summit Springs valley below, they saw the clustered lodges of Tall Bull's village. To some it looked like all the Indians in the world were there.

Carr briefly halted the command and quickly ordered a battle formation of two ranks. The General placed three companies in the first line and divided them into three parallel columns. One column under Price was placed on the right, another on the left under Walker, while the last, under Crittenden was to make the frontal assault. Crittenden was directed to take command of the first line. Carr, the war eagle, took the second line.

THE CHARGE
(Sketch by Fredric Remington)
From: DRAWINGS BY REMINGTON

CHAPTER 4

RESCUE

The Dog Soldiers were peaceful in their village. The day after their night raid on the cavalry they had gathered at Summit Springs. They had traveled hard, outrunning the relentless, determined soldiers. At last, by their tricks of the trail, they had finally eluded them. When the soldiers turned back on July 9th, they slowed their pace. Chief Tall Bull kept scouts in the south where they had last seen the cavalry. The whitemen, it seemed, were lost by the constant scattering of their trails, or had gone home. No scouts were sent to the north or west as the troops were not expected from there. The Army would have had to travel 150 miles in four days, undetected, to get ahead of them in those directions.

Before deciding to remain camped, Tall Bull had sent Two Crows and some men to check the river. They rode into the water, expecting to find it deep, but found it was only as high as their horses' backs.

They were able to cross, so they searched for a crossing which was most shallow. They marked the crossing by sticking willow poles in the sand. Upon returning to the camp that evening, they reported that the river was not as high as expected, and that a possible crossing was located. White Horse, a lesser Dog Soldier chief than Tall Bull, was unable to talk the tribe into attempting the crossing. It was too dangerous for the women and children, and they were too loaded down with plunder and equipment.

Most of Tall Bull's Cheyenne were content to take their

hard earned rest. They would keep camp in the obscure, small valley, south of the Platte River for two days. Then when the river waters went down more, they would cross over to camp on the high bluffs near the square butte, whitemen called Court House Rock, Nebraska.

There they could watch for soldiers without fear of surprise, and continue their trek through Wyoming to join Red Cloud and get to the Black Hills.

But most of the Sioux were uneasy. They believed the troops were still following their trail. When a Sioux war party returned with rumors of soldiers coming from behind, two bands under Whistler and Two Strikes quickly resolved to cross the river that night. Tall Bull stayed by his decision to remain in camp. The chiefs made plans to meet later and parted ways.

The following day was hot and smoky. The Indians had been burning grass to camouflage their trail. Everything looked indistinct. In the heat of the afternoon, the Indians rolled up the sides of their lodges so that the wind might cool them in the shade. The warriors rested and took their noon meal. Only the women moved about performing their various chores, while their children played in the nearby stream.

A few men lounged on a little hill overlooking the camp. But none saw the advancing soldiers. None sensed the danger.

Three o'clock, July 11, 1869; the Fifth Cavalry, less than a mile from the Indian Village, was still undiscovered. Wind stirred clouds of dust around them, blurring their visability and dampening the sound of their advance. Carr looked over the land, checked his men, turned and ordered, "Sound the Charge!" In the howling wind, the short, sharp bugle notes went all but unheard, but the men saw the motion. This is what they had sacrificed for, why they had made their forced, exhaustive marches. As spurs sank, horses reared high and were put at full speed. The advance became ragged as the slower horses fell behind. The irregular blue line went unnoticed until it burst into the valley where the Dog Soldiers camped. The urgent hoof beats signaled the beginning of the savage battle.

Little Hawk, who was some distance from the village, first sighted the troops. But his signals were not seen in the already smoky skies. He tried to outride the soldiers but his horse was slow. When the soldiers outraced him, he joined some fugitives from the village and got away. He lived to see may of his people killed or wounded.

An Indian boy also spotted the charge as he was tending horses. Gathering the herd before him, he drove it towards the village to warn the Indians and provide their escape. He rode hard for the village, shouting his warnings, but the wind was against him. Still, if he should reach the village in time, the Cavalry's advantage of surprise would be lost. The soldiers fired repeatedly. The boy rode on. When the herder reached camp to join in the defense of his people, he and his horse were cut down in a volley of gun fire.

Even these first sounds of attack went unnoticed by many in the village. Resting in their lodges, the Cheyenne first mistook the Pawnee soldiers, who reached the village first, for a returning Sioux war party. It was not until they saw the blue soldiers' uniforms and flashing sabers that they ran to save their women and children.

Women ran through the camp calling hysterically for their children. Some ran on foot to find hiding places in the bluffs. Those who could catch horses gave them to women with children and old people who could not fight.

As the first line of Cavalry spread destruction through the village, Price's unit took the enemy's left flank, where they killed seven warriors and captured many animals. At the same time, Captain Walker attempted to turn the enemy's right flank, though bad ground delayed him, and a number of Indians escaped. General Carr brought up the remaining companies. The battle raged around him as he searched for the women prisoners.

Troopers, with horses splashing through the stream, surrounded all but the south side of the camp. Animals stampeded in all directions. Over the Pawnee war cries and sounds of shooting, the screams of women and children could be heard. Those who could escape scattered southward across the prairie in little groups. The Pawnee followed, ruthless in their shooting and killing.

Kills Many Bulls, Two Crows and Lone Bear protected fleeing women and children. Though the other two braves were on foot, Lone Bear was mounted. Again and again he charged against the pursuing Pawnee, covering the flight of Two Crows and Kills Many Bulls as well as the women and children they were defending. When Lone Bear's horse went down, he died fighting like a wild man. His mutilated body was scalped and hacked by Pawnee tomahawks.

Tall Bull's horses had stampeded in the onslaught. He mounted one of his wives on a horse with his eight-year-old daughter and ordered her to escape. She begged him to ride with her, but he refused and sent her out of the village. He then cried out that anyone on foot, unable to get away, should follow him.

In an effort to divert the soldiers from the fleeing Indians, Tall Bull led his followers into a ravine and fought in a suicide mission. Using their tomahawks and knives, they would cut toe holes in the sides of the steep ravine so they could climb up and fire over the edge. One by one, they died. Along with their chief, who was shot in the forehead, the bodies of over a dozen Indians were found inside. Tall Bull's youngest wife, Powder Face along with his wife and son, Big Gip and his wife, and Black Moon were among those killed. Only White Buffalo Woman, eldest of Tall Bull's three wives, was allowed to surrender.

Wolf with Plenty of Hair staked himself with a dog rope at the ravine entrance. In the heat of the battle, no one had time to pull the picket pin and release him. He fought and died at his stake. This was the last known occasion when the "dog rope" was used by a Dog Soldier.

The Pawnee took every opportunity for vengeance against

their hated enemy. Women and children were killed with warriors alike. According to Luther North, Major North's younger brother, Traveling Bear, a six-foot, two hundred pound Pawnee scout, was particularly zealous in the killing. A few minutes after he entered one of the draws where a number of Cheyenne had fled, he emerged with four Cheyenne scalps and several weapons.

In the midst of the battle, Maria staggered from a lodge and grasping a soldier, pleaded with him in German. Though he did not know her language, he knew well enough her tears of anguish and the blood that stained her body. Her clothes were in rags and her skin tanned almost as dark as her captors. She led the soldiers to Susanna, who had been shot then tomahawked by Tall Bull's squaw. As the soldiers reached her, she took her last gasping breath and died.

The Indians has also attempted the young immigrant's murder, but by some miracle, the bullet through her breast had deflected off a rib. The Army surgeon, Doctor Louis Tesson, gave her immediate attention, and the wound was not fatal. An interpreter was found and Maria sobbed out her story of forty-three days of slavery, covering her face in humiliation.

Both women were pregnant and had been raped repeatedly. In Tall Bull's absence, they were constantly whipped and abused by his jealous squaws because he kept both women in his lodges. Though they had tried to make plans to escape, their language barrier had made communication almost impossible. And if they had escaped, there would have been no place to run, no place to hide in the immense empty land. They would have made easy targets in the treeless open prairie.

All the afternoon of the battle, winds had gathered force. Finally, the storm broke with thunder, lightning and hail. The soldiers took shelter in the Indian lodges, where they found countless reminders of the raided white settlements. Besides the expected arsenals and supplies, there were photograph albums, watches, jewelry, china, silverware, quilts, money and gold. Several scalps of white women were found as was a necklace made of human finger bones.

But now, they were the victorious ones. They would spend a dry night in the lodges of their enemies. They would build fires, make coffee and dine on dried buffalo meat.

Throughout the evening, troops wandered in through the raging storm. A bolt of lightning struck and killed one horse but left the rider unharmed. Around ten o'clock the wagon train came in. Of the command, only one soldier was wounded.

There was a mist from the night's rain as reveille sounded early the next morning. At daybreak troopers were sent out across the hazy hills to find any hovering Indians. The official count revealed fifty-two Indians were killed and seventeen women and children were captured.

The warm morning sun was breaking through when services were held for Susanna. The soldiers wrapped her pitiful body in lodge skins and buffalo robes. They dug a deep grave and assembled to read the burial service. Maria again broke into tears at the memory of the suffering she had shared with the dead woman. Vivid was Susanna's anguished face watching her baby being strangled then dismembered. There were few among the rugged, rough soldiers untouched by sorrow. They left a wooden headboard, marking what little they knew of Susanna.

After the conclusion of the service, Carr turned his attention to the Indian camp. He directed the troops to load everything moveable and useful on the wagons. A torch was ordered to be put to everything that remained. The whole camp of eighty-four lodges was burned. At one time the windswept plains of Summit Springs were aglow with over one hundred fifty fires.

Sending men off to Fort Sedgwick, Colorado Territory, dispatches were telegraphed to the rest of the nation. Carr's victory would make front page news in the July 15th issue of the "New York Times". Moving his Fifth Cavalry in easy marches along the South Platte River, Carr headed for Julesburg. In addition to money, the ring cut from George's finger was returned to Maria. She was made as comfortable as possible and moved by ambulance along with the troops. The Republican River Expedition was over.

THE SUMMIT SPRINGS RESCUE
(Oil by Charles Schreyvogel)
Courtesy: Buffalo Bill Historical Society, Cody, Wyoming.

CHAPTER 5

AFTERMATH

In the fall of 1869, when the rest of the world was discussing the new waterway, the Suez Canal, the Southern Cheyenne were mourning. Roman Nose was dead, Black Kettle was dead, and now Tall Bull was dead. Like the buffalo, the proud Central Plains warriors were thinning; destroyed were their dreams of complete freedom. The power of the once feared Dog Soldiers was utterly crushed. Never again would they claim their hunting grounds between the South Platte and Arkansas Rivers. A decade later, the Republican plains would no longer be a frontier. It would change from an Indian-held wilderness to a region ready for settlement.

After the Summit Springs battle, many Dog Soldiers headed South, to surrender at Camp Supply, Oklahoma. Others chose to follow White Horse, joining with the defiant Northern Cheyenne and Sioux in Wyoming. This famous warrior society, however, was defeated and after Summit Springs would not again be a factor in the wars of the Plains Indians. In January of 1875 White Horse's band surrendered. They would not participate in the Custer Battle at Little Big Horn.

The Indian prisoners were sent to the Whetstone Agency on the Missouri River.

Having completed their Republican River Expedition, the Fifth Cavalry rested for two weeks at Fort Sedgwick, Julesburg, Colorado. There they entertained themselves with billiard games and horse racing. There was heavy betting while Cody's captured Indian horse, named Tall Bull, won most of the races. Cody bragged his was the fastest running horse West of the Mississippi.

Carr planned to follow the escaped Indians up the Platte River. But when he learned that his infant son had died, he turned his command over to Colonel Royall, and the bearded war eagle went to comfort his wife in St. Louis.

Carr was to live and die an army man. He served in the 1876 Sioux campaign, the 1881 Cibicu Creek attack and the 1891 Ghost Dance uprising. He retired from the U. S. Army in 1893, and spent his later years in Washington, D.C. When he died in 1910, he was buried with full military honors in the West Point Cemetery.

William (Buffalo Bill) Cody lived his own legend. After serving as an army plains scout and acting as a hunting guide for visiting European aristocracy, the handsome buffalo hunter established his world renowned Wild West Shows. In 1907, Carr was his guest of honor at a reenactment of the Summit Springs rescue staged in Madison Square Garden. The battle had contributed to the reputations of both men. Carr was recognized as a military hero, while Cody was known as the greatest Plainsman, the greatest rifle shot from horseback of all times. For a while, he and his Summit Springs comrade, Frank North, had a cattle ranch together in Western Nebraska.

Having recovered from her wounds, Maria Weichell left Fort Sedgwick in August. According to various unsubstantiated reports, she either married the hospital attendant, a blacksmith, a Fifth Cavalry soldier, or a farmer from eastern Kansas. In any case, the beautiful, cultured immigrant vanished into the history of the Western frontier.

The Summit Springs valley remains much as it was. The wind is almost always present in its gently rolling sand hills and rugged prairie. It caresses the knoll where Susanna Alderdice lies buried. It whistles in the deep, crude ravine where Tall Bull died.

GENERAL EUGENE CARR, 1869
Courtesy: Nebraska State Historical Society, Lincoln, Nebraska.

Carr, 39 years old, commanded the U. S. 5th Cavalry from Ft. McPherson to Summit Springs. A West Point graduate and a Civil War veteran, he was a true cavalry officer who loved being in the saddle, leading his men in the field. A typical Western frontier officer, the bearded war eagle had come West to become an Indian fighter after the Civil War. Though slightly below average in height, he was straight and soldierly in appearance. His piercing eyes commanded respect. He was born and raised in the green hills and valley of Hamburg, New York.

PAWNEE INDIAN SCOUTS
Courtesy: Nebraska State Historical Society, Lincoln, Nebraska.

MAJOR FRANK NORTH, 1867
Courtesy: Nebraska State Historical Society, Lincoln, Nebraska

The Major was 29 years old at the battle of Summit Springs. He was commander of the famous Pawnee Indians, who were scouts for the U. S. Army. They called him Pa-nile-shar, Chief of the Pawnees. It was a name given only to one other white man, John Fremont, because of the great respect the Pawnee had for him.

ROMAN NOSE, CHEYENNE WAR LEADER (2ND FROM LEFT) AT FORT LARAMIE, 1867.
Courtesy: Smithsonian Institution, Washington, D.C.

A tall, muscular man with great courage, Roman Nose was an inspirational and splendid fighter, who was looked up to by most of his tribe especially the young Dog Soldiers. He possessed great influence, and though he was an acknowledged war leader of the Southern Cheyenne, he was not a chief. He believed he had magic to ward off bullets, but any metal touching his food was against his medicine. Before the famous Beecher Island Battle, when the Cheyenne had gone one day to feast with the Sioux, one of the women had used an iron fork to cook fried bread, and he did not discover this until after he had eaten the bread. His magic power to escape bullets was broken. The Forsythe scouts were discovered shortly thereafter and he could not complete his purification ceremonies before battle. Roman Nose was killed when he led a charge against the scouts.

FIFTH CAVALRY SOLDIERS, 1870.
Courtesy: Nebraska State Historical Society, Lincoln, Nebraska.

The 5th Cavalry of the U. S. Army had an international composition in 1869. Officers included several foreign born from Ireland, England, Denmark, and Germany. Most men had enlisted for financial problems, because they could not find work, to avoid the law, or to just be a soldier. For these, the West offered excitement; buffalo hunting, Indian fighting, gold mining and freedom. Their backgrounds included factory worker, farmer, drifter, businessman or immigrant. Many were soldiers from the Civil War. The rate of pay for a private was thirteen dollars a month.

CUSTER AND GRAND DUKE ALEXIS, 1872
Courtesy: Denver Public Library, Western History Department
Denver, Colorado

In 1872, Buffalo Bill was hunting guide for the 19 year-old Grand Duke Alexis of Russia. With the 7th Cavalry of the U. S. government in attendance, George Custer made up a threesome, who in their fancy buckskins, fluttered many a feminine heart at Fort Hays, Kansas. Buffalo hunting was his excuse for being in America, but the main purpose for the Duke's visit to the high plains was to make merry. The royal hunt included such things as champagne before breakfast, and throughout the day. Cody went on to become the most famous of the frontier plainsmen. General Custer and his men were annihilated by Sitting Bull at Little Big Horn.

WILLIAM (BUFFALO BILL) CODY, 1870
Courtesy: Nebraska State Historical Society, Lincoln, Nebraska

William F. Cody was born in a log cabin on an Iowa farm in 1846. His family moved to Kansas when he was eight years old. By the time Cody was eleven, he was working as a livestock herder. A short time later, he rode briefly for the pony express, which was organized by Russell, Majors and Waddell. After he was selected as a rider, and using a letter of introduction by Majors, Cody met Jack Slade, stage station boss at Julesburg, Colorado. Slade was one of the roughest, toughest characters on the frontier. His reputation had spread so far he was a landmark on the Overland Trail. At first, he balked at hiring Cody because he was so young, but finally assigned him to the stretch from Red Buttes to Three Crossings, which was one of the most hazardous of the entire pony route. Cody served in the Civil War, married when he was twenty, and was a longtime friend of Wild Bill Hickcock. With a Springfield rifle called "Lucretia Borgia," he became famous hunting buffalo for the Kansas Pacific Railroad. Buffalo Bill was chief of scouts for the U. S. Army in many Indian campaigns, including Summit Springs.

DENVER, 1870's
Courtesy: Denver Public Library, Western History Department
Denver, Colorado

The settlement was started in 1858 because of the Russell gold discovery at Cherry Creek and the South Platte. It was General Larimer, a sometime preacher who named the settlement "Denver" after the governor of Kansas, James Denver. Originally, a ferry was used to cross the South Platte River, until bridges were built. The rough, emerging, frontier town, the Queen City of the Plains, was where most newcomers from the East headed. It became the supply center for the mountains of the West. Evans was selected Governor of the territory by Lincoln in 1862. Early Denver had the fire disaster of 1863, the Cherry Creek flood in 1864, and shortly thereafter, the Plains Indians War. By 1867, Denver was considered the permanent seat of Colorado territory, having won out over Golden in the claim of being the capital. In June, the railroad was completed from Cheyenne, and in August, from Kansas; Denver, in 1870, had two rail outlets to the rest of the nation.

FORT MC PHERSON, 1870
Courtesy: Nebraska State Historical Society, Lincoln, Nebraska

FIFTH CAVALRY TROOPER, 1870
Courtesy: Nebraska State Historical Society, Lincoln, Nebraska.

PART II

CHAPTER 6

PRESS RELEASE

THE INDIAN WAR

A Cheyenne Village Surprised by Gen. Ruggles

Fifty-two Indians Killed and Seventeen Taken Prisoners

Principal Chiefs, Animals, Army and Camp Equipage Captured

Official Dispatch from Major Carr

OMAHA

(Special Dispatch to the Missouri Democrat)

OMAHA, July 13—The following has just been received:

HEADQUARTERS REPUBLICAN EXPEDITION July 12, via Fort Sedgewick, July 13.

Gen. Ruggles, A. A. G. Department of the Platte: On the 11th last, I surprised a village of Dog Soldiers and Cheyennes, under command of Tall Bull, killed 52, captured 17, women and children -- among them a wife and daughter of Tall Bull. They had two white women, taken on the Saline. They murdered one, whose first name is said to be Susanna. We gave her Christian burial. They attempted to murder Maria Welgel (sic), but the ball glanced on a rib, and she will probably recover.

The surprise was very complete for such an open country. They did not get off a single pack, left most of their saddles, and will have no shelter or food except horse meat till they can find buffalo. We captured three hundred and fifty animals, eighty-six lodges, forty rifles, twenty pistols, a number of robes, and quantities of camp equipage, which was destroyed. The names of the chiefs captured are: Good Bear, Whistler, Powder Face, Pretty Bear, Stern Face and Bull Thigh. We followed them for ten days and found them at a spring east of the South Platte, near Valley Station. They went back toward the head of Frenchman's Fork.

They still have many animals. We galloped over fifteen miles through hills of deep sand; our horses entirely gave out, and some died, they will require several weeks rest. I am coming to Fort Sedgewick.

E. A. Carr, Major 5th Cavalry
Brevet Major General Commanding

NOTES:

1. Reprinted from "Missouri Democrat", July 14, 1869.
2. A repeat of this news release was carried on the front page of the "New York Times", July 15, 1869.
3. Quantities of captured items incorrect.
4. Names of some Indian chiefs in error.

CHAPTER 7

OFFICIAL DOCUMENTS

JUNE 7, 1869 ORDERS TO GENERAL E. A. CARR

You are assigned to command the force destined to operate in the Republican Country during the present season. Your Command will consist of ten companies of the 5th Cavalry and two companies of Pawnee Scouts. You are expected to leave Fort McPherson on the morning of the 9th inst. With eight companies of the Fifth Cavalry and the Pawnee Scouts, with twenty days supplies, you will proceed to below the mouth of Dog River, scouting the country well to the north and east of your route, to be certain that no Indians are between you and the settlements in Nebraska. You will then turn west and proceed to the head waters of the Republican River, examining the country, thoroughly, on either side of your route, a distance of fifteen or twenty miles. Having well beaten up the country about the headwaters of the Republican toward Fort Sedgwick, Morgan, and Denver, you will take such other route as your knowledge of the country, the information you have acquired during your march, and other circumstances you may determine as the most promising to enable you to accomplish the purpose of the expedition, "To clear the Republican Territory of Indians." All Indians found in that country will be treated as hostile, unless they submit themselves as ready and willing to go to the proper reservation. In that event, you will disarm them, and require such hostages and guarantees of their good faith as you deem fully satisfactory. You may then bring them and their families to Fort McPherson. The two companies of the fifth cavalry left at Fort McPherson, will take out a train of twenty days supplies to meet you at Thickwood Creek or such other point as you may indicate. On your junction with this train, you will send four empty trains for additional supplies to Fort McPherson, and designate a point where it will meet you in twenty days.

You will have a journal kept and a map made of your main route, and connect with it one and all scouts and detachments therefrom. You will take every opportunity to report to me, the progress of your operations, all the information you can obtain respecting the Indians, their numbers, tribe, etc. If in following the trail of any party, you should be satisfied the Indians are to cross either Rail Road, you will notify troops along such Road and telegraph as soon as possible Department Headquarters.

These instructions are of course of the most general character. The object of your expedition is to drive the Indians out of the Republican Country and to follow them as far as possible. Most of the details of the operation must be left to your judgment.

The Department Commander relies upon your known energy and skill to accomplish successfully a result so important.

Official letter to:
Brevet General E. A. Carr, Commander of the 5th Cavalry
By Command of General Auger
Headquarters Department of the Platte, Omaha, Nebraska
Signed by George D. Ruggles, Assist. Adjutant General

CARR'S OFFICIAL RECORD — JULY 20, 1869

I have the honor respectfully to submit the following report of the operations of my command since my last communication dated "Camp on Buffalo Head Creek," June 30th, 1869.

The creek proves to have been previously named Porcupine Creek.

In that letter I reported a trail about a week old going up the Republican.

I also reported that the supply train escort under Major Crittenden had seen Indians on the McPherson road the day previous to their arrival at my camp. I sent Major Crittenden and the two companies he brought with him, with some Pawnees, to follow those Indians, but they were found to have been a herd of Buffalo.

Meantime, I sent a party of Pawnees to follow the first trail and found where the Indians had encamped and pulled off many mule shoes.

Upon the return of Major Crittenden's command, I proceeded up the Republican, taking the North Fork, and sending parties of Pawnees to follow the trail, and report its direction.

It seemed to follow the general course of the North Fork of the Republican, keeping, however about ten miles away from that stream, and encamping on the heads of small tributaries.

It was reported as about thirty lodges, with about three hundred animals. They were moving with the greatest precautions to avoid pursuit.

They would scatter when leaving camp; then come together on the high, hard prairie and drive their animals in every direction to confuse the trail; then scatter again and not reassemble till near their night camp.

On the 4th day of July, believing that the Indians were near, I sent Bvt. Colonel W. B. Royall with three companies 5th Cavalry and one of Pawnee Scouts amounting to about one hundred men, with three days rations, to follow the trail. His orders were to try to surprise them, kill as many warriors as possible and capture their families and animals.

Colonel Royall travelled 38 miles the first day, and sent in an express reporting that the trail was four days old and going north.

He was then sixteen miles from North Fork.

Next day he followed the trail 18 miles to the northward when the Pawnees caught sight of a war party of 12, with one on a litter.

The Pawnees reported that the "*Whole Party*" was there and started in pursuit; and the troops had no choice but to follow. They killed three and dispersed the rest, wounding some.

The chase led them so far back towards the point of starting, that Colonel Royall concluded to rejoin the command, as he had but one more day's rations, and believed that the main trail was at least four days old, and that the Indians had been alarmed by those already encountered.

Meantime, I had moved by easy marches up the North Fork of the Republican. Had run out the water on Rock Creek and encamped on the head of Black Tail Deer Creek intending to strike from there south and scout the other branches.

I found that the waters of North Fork do not extend as far westward as represented on the map.

Colonel Royall rejoined me on the 7th and I determined to take the whole command and follow the trail. My instructions being to scout the country towards Forts Sedgwick and Morgan, and Denver, I thought best to follow the order named in them; and the trail being reported so old, and the Indians being alarmed, and, it being probable that it would require a chase too long for rations to be carried without wagons.

I had little hope of overtaking the Indians, but thought I could at least hunt them out of the country.

I moved down the North Fork one day's march in order to get a practicable road to the trail.

During the day three men of Company "M" who were several miles in rear of the column bringing in a given-out horse, were attacked by eight Indians. They got near a large rock for a breastwork on one side, and killed the horse as a defense on the other; and beat off the Indians wounding two badly.

Corporal John Kyle, Co. "M" 5th Cavalry was in charge of

the party; he showed especial bravery on this, as he had done on previous occasions.

About midnight, an attack was made on our camp by a number of Indians, who charged in among the horses, yelling, and firing into camp. They did not succeed in getting any animals or injuring any one.

Sergeant Co-rux-te-chod-ish (Mad Bear) Pawnee, who was Sergeant of the Pawnee guard, ran out after one of the Indians whose horse had fallen and thrown him and was about to overtake and kill him when he was shot down by a bullet from our own side. He is slowly recovering from his wound.

He deserves special mention for this and also for killing two of those killed by Col. Royall's command.

On the 9th I moved northward, made a very long, hot and tiresome day's march through sand hills, and encamped on water holes or lakes near where Colonel Royall had left the trail.

Next day followed the trail which led up Frenchman's Fork, passed two of their camps and encamped on a third, which I judged from the map to be about fifteen miles from Valley Station on the South Platte.

They had left it that morning and I determined to leave the wagons and push for them.

I took all available men; that is, all those whose horses were fit for service and they amounted to two hundred and forty four (244) officers and soldiers and fifty (50) Pawnees out of seven companies 5th Cavalry and one hundred and fifty Pawnees.

This shows the necessity of having the horses well fed and cared for and of having extra animals on every expedition.

On the 11th instant, I started with the above command, and three day's rations; leaving the train to follow as rapidly as it could.

During the morning we had two reports of Indians in front, and took up the gallop; but they turned out to be wild horses.

Frenchman's Fork runs very far up towards the South Platte.

It has several branches which mostly appear to be streams of sand; but the water sometimes appears on the surface, and can always be found in plenty by digging a few inches with the hands.

When we reached the breaks of the Platte Bluffs the Pawnees reported seeing two horsemen; and recommended taking the whole command into a ravine; which was done.

The trail appeared to divide here, a small portion going to the right, but the main part keeping to the left on the table land.

Taking for granted, however, that it must go to the Platte for water, of which we were also in much need, I moved directly towards that stream through bad sand for several miles; when a report was brought in of a herd of animals in the valley near the stream to the right, while at the same time came a report from the left of mounted Indians seen.

I determined to detach Colonel Royall with three companies, to move direct for the animals; and, with the rest move towards where the Indians were reported, as that was the direction of the main trail. I sent the pack mules back to the train which was in sight, and both parties struck out on a gallop. In a few minutes I received information that "tepees" had been seen in the direction I was pursuing; I sent to Colonel Royall to send me a company as soon as he could spare one; and he promptly sent me his strongest company.

We galloped about an hour through low sand hills and loose sand, and saw no signs of Indians, and I began to think the whole was a humbug, and that I would have to follow them across the Platte and across the Railroad to the north, when some Pawnees beckoned me to come to them, which I did with the command, though with little hope of finding anything.

It was now after two P.M. and the animals had had no water since morning, and had been travelling rapidly for a long distance through the hot, loose sand.

The Pawnees pointed out a herd of animals about four

miles off in the hills. Having been so often disappointed I thought it very possible it might be Buffalo, but, of course, determined to go and see.

The Pawnees stripped themselves for the fight; taking off their saddles and as much of their clothing as could be dispensed with and still leave something to distinguish them from the hostiles.

About this time Colonel Royall rejoined with his command, having found that the animals reported were bushes. He had travelled nearly twenty miles through the sand.

We kept in the depressions between the sand hills, moving at a rapid gait.

When concealment was no longer possible I placed the three leading companies in parallel columns of twos, directed Major Crittenden, 5th Cavalry, to take command and sounded the charge.

We were then over a mile from the village and still undiscovered.

The leading companies with the Pawnees on their left, put their horses at speed while the rest followed at a fast gallop. Of course the advance was much scattered owing to the difference in the speed of the horses. But some of them reached the village so quickly that the Indians had little time to saddle or bridle their horses or to get their arms; and many of them could not even get on horseback.

The attack was made from the northwest, the valley in which they were encamped running west.

Those whose bands of horses were up the heads of ravines to the eastward mostly drove them off as they ran, but we got all which were below the village and most which were near it.

An Indian, among those who were trying to get off the lower herd, when he found it was too late to do so, attempted to pass himself off as a squaw; and finding that would not do, attempted to parley, saying, "Me good Indian, talk heap." But, of course it would not do to wait and let the others escape.

Tall Bull, the chief, finding how matters were going, determined to die. He had a little daughter on his horse and one of his wives on another. He gave the daughter to his wife and told her to escape and take the white woman who was prisoner, and she might use her to make terms for herself when peace was made. The wife begged him to escape with her, but he shut his ears, killed his horse, and she soon saw him killed, fighting.

She then surrendered and was saved with her daughter of 8, and brother of 12 years.

As the ground was developed, I sent in the remaining companies. The troops charged through the village, and pursued for about four miles beyond; some of their horses giving out at every step, until finally none were able to raise a gallop.

They then slowly returned towards the village, driving in the captured stock.

There were two white women in the village, one of whom they murdered, and the other they attempted to murder; but we were too quick for them and she escaped with a painful wound. As the troops came in, I posted pickets, laid out the camp so as to include the village, and sent for the train which had gone to the Platte; it arrived in camp about ten at night.

I also detailed a Board to ascertain the number of killed and prisoners and the amount of captures.

It stormed considerably during the afternoon and evening; one horse was killed by lightning. Next morning I sent parties in every direction to see if any Indians were hovering about, count dead bodies, and drive in stray animals; caused to be gathered and loaded such property as could be carried, and had the remainder burned. There were 160 fires burning at once to destroy this property.

The report, of the Board herewith enclosed gives the amounts in detail.

The main items are, fifty-two killed on the field, seventeen women and children captured, 274 horses and 144 mules captured, twenty-five killed, ninety-three hundred (9300) pounds dried meat, eighty-four (84) lodges, complete, fifty-six (56) rifles, twenty-two (22) revolvers, forty (40) bows with arrows, fifty (50) lbs. powder, twenty (20) lbs. bullets, eight (8) bars lead, fourteen (14) bullet moulds, twenty-five (25) boxes (12000) Percussion caps, seventeen (17) Sabres, nine (9) lances and twenty (20) tomahawks. There is much other valuable property on the list, but the above will materially reduce their means of killing white people.

They prove to be Dog Soldiers; Cheyennes and Ogallallah Sioux. I had only one man slightly scratched by an arrow.

I lost one (1) horse killed by the enemy and twelve (12) died in the chase.

The Pawnees under Major Frank North were of the greatest service to us throughout the campaign. This is the first time since coming west, that we have been supplied with Indian scouts -- and the result has shown their value.

The place where the battle took place, is, I believe, called "Summit Springs".

It is a source of extreme gratification to the 5th Cavalry that, after all our hardships and exposures for ten months in the field, we have at last met with an undisputed success.

We undoubtedly drove the main village of 800 lodges out of Kansas in October last, which gave peace to that State during the winter; we spent a most miserable and depressing winter on the Canadian, watching our base, and we chased these same Indians in May and fought them twice, losing four (4) killed and several wounded. It may be imagination, but there is a general feeling that the services and hardships of the Regiment have not been appreciated for want of any brilliant list of killed and wounded.

We have however, no pleasure in killing the poor miserable savages; but desire, in common with the whole army, by the performance of our duty, to deliver the settlers from the dangers to which they are exposed on account of the past mistaken policy, or rather want of policy, in Indian affairs; which renders it necessary to chastise them until they submit.

I have, as usual, to express my obligations to the officers

and soldiers of my command for their energy, activity, and cheerful endurance of hardships.

I may mention as of especial assistance to me, 1st Lieut. Jacob Almy, Adjutant, 1st Lieut. E. P. Doherty, A.A.I.M., and 2nd Lieut. Wm. J. Volkmar, Acting Topographical and Signal Officer.

On account of the exhausted condition of my animals, and the large quantity of loose stock, I came in to this Post; where I propose to remain for two or three weeks to rest my animals, and cure sore backs.

The white woman who was murdered was no doubt Mrs. Susan Alderdice. Doctor Louis S. Tesson, of St. Louis, Acting Assistant Surgeon, examined her, and states that she answers the description sent by Mr. Alderdice. She had a babe which the Indians strangled after three days.

We wrapped her in lodge skins and robes, and dug a deep grave; the officers and soldiers were assembled, and the burial service was read over her.

A head board marks the grave with an inscription stating what we knew of her. The name of the rescued woman is Mrs. Maria Wiechell from Lüneberg, Hanover, Germany. She had been married two years and had been but two months in this country. She was taking a Sunday afternoon walk with her husband and some friends when the Indians appeared. Her husband was killed before her eyes, and his finger cut off for a ring.

Both women were pregnant and both were no doubt raped by a dozen of the savages.

My men donated most of the captured money to Mrs. Wiechell, amounting to eight hundred and forty-five dollars and thirty-five cents ($845.35) in national currency and four twenty dollar gold pieces. She was well cared for; a tent was assigned to her use and she was carried in our easiest ambulance. She is now in the Post Hospital and in a fair way for recovery.

I enclose papers captured which certify to the high character of certain Indians, who must have greatly degenerated since they were written.

There was a necklace captured, formed of human fingers; also scalps of white women, articles of household furniture, such as clocks, quilts, etc.

I have a Board in session to examine the claims of persons who present themselves as owners of captured stock, and will turn over such as may be identified.

Official letter to:
Brevet Brigadier General George D. Ruggles, Assist. Adjutant General
Headquarters Department of the Platte, Omaha, Nebraska
By Bvt. Major General (5th Cavalry) E. A. Carr
Headquarters Republican River Expedition Camp
near Fort Sedgwick, Colorado territory.

SPECIAL ORDERS NO. 17 — JULY 11, 1869

Bvt. Col. W. B. Royall, Major 5th Cavalry, Major E. W. Crittenden, 5th Cavalry, 2nd Lieut. R. A. Edwards, 5th Cavalry, are hereby constituted a Board to ascertain and report the number of Indians killed and the number of Indians and amounts of property captured, particularly the number of Horses, Mules, Lodges, Arms, and quantity of Provisions.

The Board will convene immediately and finish its duties as soon as practicable.

The junior member will act as recorder.
By order of Bvt. Maj. Gen. E. A. Carr
REPUBLICAN RIVER EXPEDITION
Signed by J. Almy (Actg. Adj.)

CAMP REPUBLICAN RIVER EXPEDITION, JULY 11, 1869

The Board met pursuant the above order.
Present all the members.
The Board proceeded to examine into the amount of Indian

property captured and destroyed in today's fight with a Camp of eighty four (84) lodges of dog soldiers and Sioux and find after careful investigation the following list to be correct:

56 Rifles
22 Revolvers
40 Sets Bows & Arrows
20 Tomahawks
47 Axes
150 Knives
50 lbs. Powder
20 lbs. Bullets
14 Bullet Moulds
8 Bars Lead
25 Box Perc. Caps
17 Sabres
17 War Shields
9 Lances
13 War Bonnets
690 Buffalo Robes
552 Panniers
152 Moccasins
319 Raw Hides
361 Saddles
31 Mess Pans
52 Water Kegs
67 Brass/Iron Camp Kettles
200 Raw Hide Lariats

16 bottles Strychnine
84 Lodges, complete
125 Travois
9300 lbs. Meat, dried
160 Tin Cups
180 Tin Plates
200 Dressing Knives
8 Shovels
75 Lodge Skins (new)
40 Saddle Bags
75 Bridles
28 Womans Dresses (new)
50 Hammers
9 Coats
100 lbs. Tobacco
200 Coffee Pots (Tin)
1500 Dolls
Money in Gold & Nat. Bank Notes

Horses	274
Mules	144
TOTAL	418

Horses/mules killed = 25

Besides the above mentioned articles the Board is of the opinion that there was at least ten (10) tons of various Indian property such as Clothing, Flour, Coffee, Corn Meal, Saddle Equipments, Fancy Articles, etc. etc. destroyed by the command before leaving the Camp by burning.

There were also found in the different lodges, articles which had undoubtedly been stolen from white settlements. Albums, containing photographs, daguerretypes, watches, cloaks, crokery ware, silver forks and spoons, etc. etc.

In making examination preparatory to burning the Camp quite a number of white scalps were found attached to wearing apparel, lances and childrens toys, some of which appeared to be very fresh.

There were in the engagement fifty two (52) Indians killed, the bodies of which were found and seventeen (17) women and children captured, together with one white woman, captured by these Indians on the Saline Creek, Kansas, about six weeks since named Mary (Weigel) Weichell, her husband having been killed by them; another white woman named Susanna ____________________, captured at the same time was tomahawked and killed by these Indians when the attack on the Camp commenced. The Indians also shot Mrs. (Weigel) Weichell, in the side and probably left her for dead, but she is now with the command and expected to recover.

There being no other business before them, the Board adjourned sine die.

(Signed)
W. B. Royall, Major
E. W. Crittenden, Major
Robert Edwards, 2nd Lieut.
(Recorder)

FT. SEDGWICK POST RECORDS — JULY 1869

A remarkable storm of wind, hail and rain crossed the locality of the post on the 13th last. It surpassed anything of the kind for severity, known by the persons longest in the country. Six buildings were unroofed and one animal killed by the falling roofing, no person was hurt.

Bvt. Major General E. A. Carr, Major 5th Cavalry, Command of the Republican Expedition arrived on July 21st, after a most successful expedition against the South Cheyennes, under their Chief Tall Bull. Fifty-two Indians were killed and a large amount of stock captured, together with arms. The Command will leave August 2nd, 1869 on another campaign.

GENERAL ORDERS NO. 48 — AUGUST 3, 1869

The General Commanding the Department takes pleasure in announcing to his command the success of the operations conducted by Brevet Major General E. A. Carr, Major 5th Cavalry, against the hostile indians in the "Republican country."

General Carr's command consisted of Companies "A," "C," "D," "E," "G," "H," "I," and "M," 5th Cavalry, under Majors Royall and Crittenden, and one hundred and fifty Pawnee Scouts, under Major Frank North.

Striking the Republican river near mouth of Dog Creek, General Carr turned west and followed up the general course of that stream, covering the country with his scouting parties, and severely punishing several attempts of the indians to stampede his animals. Persistently keeping his course over swollen streams and heavy sand hills for nearly three hundred miles, by good and careful management he succeeded in surprising and capturing, at Summit Springs, the entire village and property of the hostile band, including most of their animals, killing fifty-two of their number, and taking fifteen women and children prisoners. Two white captives, Mrs. Weichel and Mrs. Alderdice, were recaptured, though not in time to prevent the indians from killing the latter and wounding the former.

General Carr commends the cheerful readiness and good conduct generally of all the officers and men of the 5th Cavalry, and also of the Pawnee Scouts, under Major Frank North. He mentions especially the bravery and gallant conduct of Corporal John Kyle, Company "M," 5th Cavalry, and of Sergeant Co-rux-te-chod-ish (Mad Bear) of the Pawnee Scouts.

The General Commanding tenders his thanks to General Carr and his command, for their patient endurance of the privations and hardships inseparable from an indian campaign, and for the vigor and persistency of their operations, so deserving the success achieved.

The following embraces but a portion of the property captured: Two hundred and seventy-four horses, one hundred and forty-four mules, nine thousand three hundred pounds of dried meat, eighty-four lodges complete, fifty-six rifles; twenty-two revolvers, forty bows and arrows, fifty pounds of powder, etc., etc.

About fifteen hundred dollars in money was found in the camp by soldiers, and the General Commanding commends, in the warmest terms, the generous hearted feeling which prompted them to give most of it -- over nine hundred dollars -- to the liberated white captive Mrs. Weichel.

By Command of General Augur
Headquarters Department of the Platte, Omaha Nebraska,
Signed by George D. Ruggles

SUMMIT SPRINGS RESOLUTION — COLORADO

Whereas the prosperity of this Territory has been greatly retarded during the several years past by Indian warfare, preventing immigration; and whereas, defenseless women and children of our pioneer settlements have been murdered by savages, or subjected to captivity worse than death, and whereas, a detachment of United States troops under General Eugene Carr, on the twelfth (12th) day of July last, at Summit Springs (Weld County), in this territory, after a long and tedious pursuit, achieved a signal victory over a band of Dog Indians, retaking considerable property that had been stolen, and recaptured a white woman held captive. RESOLVED, that the thanks of the people of Colorado, through the Council and House of Representatives of the Legislative Assembly of the Territory of Colorado, be extended to Brevet Major General Eugene A. Carr, of the United States Army, and the brave officers and soldiers of his command for their victory thus achieved. RESOLVED, that the Secretary of this Territory be required to have a copy of these resolutions prepared upon parchment, and transmitted to General Carr. January 25, 1870.

SUMMIT SPRINGS RESOLUTION — NEBRASKA

RESOLVED, by the Legislature of the State of Nebraska, that the thanks of the people of Nebraska, be and are hereby tendered to Brevet Major-General Carr and the officers and soldiers under his command of the 5th U. S. Cavalry for their heroic courage and perseverance in their campaign against hostile Indians on the frontier of the State in July, 1869, driving the enemy from our borders and achieving a victory at Summit Springs, Colorado Territory, by which the people of the State were freed from the ravages of merciless savages.

2d. RESOLVED, That the thanks of this body and of the people of the State of Nebraska, are hereby also tendered to Major Frank J. North and the officers and soldiers under his command of the "Pawnee scouts" for the manner in which they have assisted in driving hostile Indians from our frontier settlements.

3d. RESOLVED, That the Secretary of State is hereby instructed to transmit a copy of the foregoing resolutions to Major-General Eugene A. Carr and Major Frank J. North. Approved, February 28, 1870.

CHAPTER 8

EYEWITNESS REMINISCENCES

THE FRANK NORTH DIARY

"Saturday 10 (July 1869) -- this morn moved at 6 a.m. and followed Indian trail 35 miles passed three of the Indians camps. water poor. in the morn we move early and take 3 days rations on pack mules and light out for the Indians. we will have a fight tomorrow sure. I hope we may come out victorious. I shall be careful for the sake of dear ones at home.

"Sunday 11 -- Marched this morn at 6 a.m. with 50 of my men and 200 whites with 3 days rations followed trail till 3 p.m. and came up to the village made a grand charge and it was a complete victory took the whole village about 85 lodges killed about 60 Indians took 17 prisoners and about 300 ponies and Robes etc. innumerables rained pretty hard tonight.

"Monday 12, 1869 -- Invoiced property today and burned what we did not want and started on the march at 12 m. for the Platte River arrived in camp at 4 p.m. find good grass and plenty of wood such as telegraph poles. we are 65 miles from Julesburgh. George and ten men went to Julesburgh with dispatches.

"Tuesday 13 -- Marched at 6:30 a.m. this morn came down the Platte 21 miles camp at River Side Fred's old stage station. good feed plent(y) wood. the Officers of the 5th Cav. selected all the best ponies and kept them. I have in charge 180 ponies don't know what will be done with them.

"Wednesday 14 -- Marched at 6:30 a.m. came down to

antelope station on the Platte distance 20 miles. nothing of importance transpired today. roads good. Gus with 4 men goes to Sedgewick tonight at midnight I telegraph home also write. I hope I can go home in a few days.

"Thursday 15 -- Marched this morn at 6 a.m. and arrived at Sedgewick at 12 m. found a very poor kept post. did not visit the post tonight. will go up in the morn

"Friday 16 -- This morn went up to the Fort and had 1 game of Billiards and came to Camp just in time to see Gen. Auger. we had a council today with the prisoners. the Gen. will take them to Omaha. divided the ponies tonight."

FROM "The Journal of An Indian Fighter -- The 1869 Diary of Major Frank J. North", edited by Donald F. Danker, published in *Nebraska History,* Volume 39, Number 2, June, 1958, the Nebraska State Historical Society. Frank North was 29 years old at the time of the battle and was commander of the Pawnee Indians, who were scouts for the U.S. Army.

THE CAPTAIN SAM SUMNER ACCOUNT

"We left the Republican River four days since to follow an Indian trail. Made long, hard marches over very rough country, but every one kept up well and pushed ahead, as the signs of Indians thickened as we proceeded. Yesterday morning we cut loose from our train, and after marching ten or twelve miles, the scouts reported a large village ahead. General Carr lengthened out at a gallop, and you never saw cavalry go it as we did for about ten miles. No signs ahead, and we were commencing to think our lookouts mistaken, when they motioned us to come further to the left. We went over, and sure enough there were their herds grazing about two miles off. The regiment was got together behind a ridge, which completely screened us, the Pawnees on the left, nearest the village, Company D next, Companies C, H, A, G, and K on the right. At the command from the General, we all started with a rush. The Indians on my left had stripped for the fight, and went in like red devils. I was ordered to keep up with them. We could not see the village, and were riding for the herd, but on reaching the top of the next ridge there lay the village a little to our left and front. You never heard such a shout; the way we rode for it was a caution. Every company tried to get there first, but I had the advantage of being the nearest. The Pawnees were with me, and, seeing themselves supported, put right ahead. It was a magnificent sight to see the Regulars rushing ahead at a run. The Indians we attacked were Dog Soldiers, the worst rascals on the Plains. They are the same band that General Carr fought in May, and the same ones that committed the depredations in Kansas some six weeks since. They were moving west with their stock and property, and had camped to rest, feeling secure in their out-of-the-way camp. They were taken completely by surprise, and did not have time to get anything away but some stock. I expected they would fight for their pillage, but they made only a feeble effort to stop us. We rushed through the village on to the hills after them, about five miles, when we gave up the chase, as our horses had given out. There never was a more complete Indian triumph on the Plains. We killed seventy-three*, captured seventeen women and children, 500 head of stock, and their whole outfit. They left their lodges standing, with everything in and around them, and this was all accomplished without the loss of a single man on our side. We had great times after our return, hunting up Indian curiosities, etc.

"July 14 -- We are now on our way to Fort Sedgwick, but have so many horses, etc., that we are compelled to march slowly. The General expects to reach there the morning of the 16th."

FROM: The *Army and Navy Journal,* Volume VI, August, 1869, page 802. It was originally printed in The Winona, Miss., "Republican", 1869, and is from a letter written by Brevet Major S. A. Sumner, captain Fifth Cavalry, to a friend in Winona. The letter is dated "Camp of Fifth Cavalry, North Platte River, fifty miles above Fort Sedgwick, July 12, 1869."

* Error.

THE WILLIAM "BUFFALO BILL" CODY ACCOUNT

"Next morning the command, at an early hour, started out to take up this Indian trail which they followed for two days as rapidly as possible; it becoming evident from the many camp fires which we passed, that we were gaining on the Indians. Wherever they had encamped we found the print of a woman's shoe, and we concluded that they had with them some white captive. This made us all the more anxious to overtake them, and General Carr accordingly selected all his best horses, which could stand a hard run, and gave orders for the wagon train to follow as fast as possible, while he pushed ahead on a forced march. At the same time I was ordered to pick out five or six of the best Pawnees, and go on in advance of the command, keeping ten or twelve miles ahead on the trail, so that when we overtook the Indians we could find out the location of their camp, and send word to the troops before they came in sight, thus affording ample time to arrange a plan for the capture of the village.

"After having gone about ten miles in advance of the regiment, we began to move very cautiously, as were now evidently nearing the Indians. We looked carefully over the summits of the hills before exposing ourselves to plain view, and at last we discovered the village, encamped in the sand-hills south of the South Platte River at Summit Springs. Here I left the Pawnee scouts to keep watch, while I went back and informed General Carr that the Indians were in sight.

"The General at once ordered his men to tighten their saddles and otherwise prepare for action. Soon all was excitement among the officers and soldiers, every one being anxious to charge the village. I now changed my horse for old Buckskin Joe, who had been led for me thus far, and was comparatively fresh. Acting on my suggestion, the General made a circuit to the north, believing that if the Indians had their scouts out, they would naturally be watching in the direction whence they had come. When we had passed the Indians and were between them and the Platte River, we turned to the left and started toward the village.

"By this maneuver we had avoided discovery by the Sioux* scouts, and we were confident of giving them a complete surprise. Keeping the command wholly out of sight, until we were within a mile of the Indians, the General halted the advance guard until all closed up, and then issued an order, that, when he sounded the charge, the whole command was to rush into the village.

"As we halted on the top of the hill overlooking the camp of the unsuspecting Indians, General Carr called out to his buglar: 'Sound the charge!' The bugler for a moment became intensely excited, and actually forgot the notes. The General again sang out: 'Sound the charge!' and yet the bugler was unable to obey the command. Quartermaster Hays -- who had obtained permission to accompany the expedition -- was riding near the General, and comprehending the dilemma of the man, rushed up to him, jerked the bugle from his hands and sounded the charge himself in clear and distinct notes. As the troops rushed forward, he threw the bugle away, then drawing his pistols, was among the first men that entered the village.

"The Indians had just driven up their horses and were preparing to make a move of the camp, when they saw the soldiers coming down upon them. A great many of them succeeded in jumping upon their ponies, and leaving everything behind them, advanced out of the village and prepared to meet the charge; but upon second thought they quickly concluded that it was useless to try to check us, and, those who were mounted rapidly rode away, while the others on foot fled for safety to the neighboring hills. We went through their village shooting right and left at everything we saw. The Pawnees, the regular soldiers and the officers were all mixed up together, and the Sioux* were flying in every direction.

"General Carr had instructed the command that when they entered the village, they must keep a sharp look out for white women, as he was confident the Indians had some captives. The company which had been ordered to take possession of the village after its capture, soon found two white women, one of whom had just been killed and the other wounded. They were both Swedes*, and the survivor could not talk English. A Swedish soldier, however, was soon found who could talk with her. The name of this woman was Mrs. Weichel, and her story as told to the soldier was, that as soon as the Indians saw the troops coming down upon them, a squaw -- Tall Bull's wife -- had killed Mrs. Alderdice, the other captive, with a hatchet, and then wounded her. This squaw had evidently intended to kill both women to prevent them from telling how cruelly they had been treated.

"The attack lasted but a short time, and the Indians were driven several miles away. The soldiers then gathered in the herd of Indian horses, which were running at large over the country and drove them back to camp. After taking a survey of what we had accomplished, it was found that we had killed about one hundred and forty* Indians, and captured one hundred and twenty* squaws and papooses, two hundred* lodges, and eight hundred* horses and mules. The village proved to be one of the richest I had ever seen. The red-skins had everything pertaining to an Indian camp, besides numerous articles belonging to the white settlers whom they had killed on the Saline. The Pawnees, as well as the soldiers, ransacked the camp for curiosities, and found enough to start twenty museums, besides a large amount of gold and silver. This money had been stolen from the Swedish settlers whom they had murdered on the Saline. General Carr ordered that all the tepees, the Indian lodges, buffalo robes, all camp equipage and provisions, including dried buffalo meat, amounting to several tons, should be gathered in piles and burned. A grave was dug in which the dead Swedish* woman, Mrs. Alderdice, was buried. Captain Kane, a religious officer, read the burial service, as we had no chaplain with us.

"While this was going on, the Sioux* warriors having recovered from their surprise, had come back and a battle took place all around the camp. I was on the skirmish line, and I noticed an Indian, who was riding a large bay horse, and giving orders to his men in his own language -- which I could occasionally understand -- telling them that they had lost everything, that they were ruined, and he entreated them to follow him, and fight until they died. His horse was an extraordinary one, fleet as the wind, dashing here and there, and I determined to capture him if possible, but I was afraid to fire at the Indian for fear of killing the horse.

"I noticed that the Indian, as he rode around the skirmish line, passed the head of a ravine not far distant, and it occurred to me that if I could dismount and creep to the ravine, I could, as he passed there, easily drop him from his saddle without danger of hitting the horse. Accordingly I crept into and secreted myself in the ravine, reaching the place unseen by the Indians, and I waited there until Mr. Chief came riding by.

"When he was not more than thirty yards distant I fired, and the next moment he tumbled from his saddle, and the horse kept on without his rider. Instead of running toward the Indians, however, he galloped toward our men, by one of whom he was caught. Lieutenant Mason, who had been very conspicuous in the fight and who had killed two or three Indians himself, single-handed, came galloping up to the ravine and jumping from his horse, secured the fancy war bonnet from the head of the dead chief, together with all his other accoutrements. We both then rejoined the soldiers, and I at once went in search of the horse; I found him in the possession of Sergeant McGrath, who had caught him. The Sergeant knew that I had been trying to get the animal and having seen me kill his rider, he handed him over to me at once.

"Little did I think at that time that I had captured a horse which, for four years afterwards was the fastest runner in the state of Nebraska, but such proved to be the fact. I jumped on his back and rode him down to the spot where the prisoners were corraled. One of the squaws among the prisoners suddenly began crying in a pitiful and hysterical manner at the sight of this horse, and upon inquiry I found that she was Tall Bull's wife, the same squaw that had killed one of the white women and wounded the other. She stated that this was her husband's favorite war-horse, and that only a short time ago she had seen Tall Bull riding him. I gave her to understand that her liege lord had passed his mortal chips and that it would be sometime before he would ride his favorite horse again, and I informed her that henceforth I should call the gallant steed 'Tall Bull', in honor of her husband."

FROM: *The Autobiography of Buffalo Bill,* 1879, Hartford, Connecticut, Frank E. Bliss, published when Cody was thirty-two, ten years after the battle. Cody's book was dedicated to General Phillip H. Sheridan.

* Error

THE GEORGE F. PRICE ACCOUNT

"About this time it became known that the enemy held as captives two white women whom they had captured on the Solomon* River about the 1st of June, and as it was evident that they were preparing to march northward, by the way of the Laramie Plains and the Black Hills of Wyoming, to the Powder River country, it became a matter of the utmost importance to intercept them and rescue the unfortunate women before they could cross the South Platte River.

"Major Carr accordingly pushed his Pawnee scouts forward, and, having ascertained the general direction in which the Indians were retreating, moved his command by rapid marches beyond their right flank, and gained a position in their front from which he was enabled to strike a blow that almost annihilated them. To accomplish this brilliant result forced marches were made until the evening of the 10th, when the troopers encamped on Frenchman's Fork, about twenty-four hours behind the enemy. About two o'clock A.M. of the 11th three squadrons (A, C, D, E, G, H) and the Pawnee scouts -- leaving Company M to escort the wagon-train -- renewed the pursuit, which was continued until the South Platte River was seen from the bluffs on the south side. A squadron (E and G) with one hundred scouts, under Major Royall, were dispatched on a reconnaissance along the river-bank to ascertain if the enemy had succeeded in effecting a crossing, although it was believed that their right flank had been turned and that they were then to the left rear of the column. This belief was soon confirmed by the arrival of the guide, William F. Cody, who reported large herds of ponies about six miles distant in a south-westerly direction, which was indubitable evidence that Tall Bull and his warriors were encamped and unconscious of approaching peril, as the pickets, who were watching their rear, had made no danger signals, and the possibility of a successful flank movement never occurred to them, because it did not seem practicable for the cavalry to march one hundred and fifty miles in four days and pass their flank without being discovered.

"When the position of the village was reasonably located Major Carr made a detour towards the north-west, and marched rapidly behind ridges and through ravines until about half-past one o'clock P.M., when he halted the cavalry about six miles south of the old Valley Station on the South Platte River and one mile north of Summit Springs, where the village was supposed to be located. The ground between the troopers and the Springs was an open plain, and the plan of the attack was soon arranged. Captain Walker, with his company, was assigned to the left, and Lieutenant Price, with Company A, was assigned to the right. They were instructed to turn the enemy's flanks, dash to the rear, and capture the herds, which could be plainly seen grazing on a hillside about two miles south, and, as was rightly conjectured, also south of the village. Captains Sumner and Maley, with their companies and the Pawnee scouts, were to charge upon the enemy's front. Company A had first to move about five hundred yards to the right for position, and Major Carr waited until Lieutenant Price signaled that he was ready, when the line moved forward at a slow trot until it appeared upon the level of the plain and about twelve hundred yards from the village. At this moment an Indian, superbly mounted on a white pony, was seen to dash from the herd. He had discovered the cavalry and instantly recognized the supreme peril of the hour. His direct and terrific pace informed Major Carr exactly where to deliver his blow, and it was of the utmost importance to strike the village before the warriors could be informed of the approaching danger. A hard gale from the west prevented the Indians in the village from hearing the noise made by the advancing line of cavalry, while the warning shouts of the herder who was riding a race with death counted as nothing against the fury of the winds. It was a moment of intense suspense. If only one Indian should chance to appear on the edge of the plain and discover the troopers, the advantage gained by the forced march and brilliant flank movement would be instantly lost; or if the herder should gain the village but one minute before the advancing cavalry could strike it, the advantage arising from a complete surprise would also be lost. The herder had not advanced twenty yards towards the village when the chief trumpeter was ordered to sound the charge. Only those who were near him could hear the short, sharp notes, but every man saw him going through the motions. That was enough. All knew that there was only one call to sound then; and away dashed the gallant troopers in one of the most superb charges ever made by the Fifth Cavalry. The spurs sunk deep in the flanks of the good but jaded horses, who, seeming to understand the necessity of the occasion, responded with a magnificent burst of speed.

"As the herder came on the edge of the ravine on the south side the troopers appeared on the edge of the ravine on the north side, and there was the prize only fifty yards from the charging line, and with ringing cheers the regiment struck the doomed village. Lieutenant Price turned the enemy's left flank, and, dashing to the rear, killed seven warriors and captured three hundred animals. Captains Sumner and Maley charged through the village and drove everything before them. Captain Walker, while endeavoring to turn the enemy's right flank, encountered an ugly side-ravine, which delayed his progress and premitted a number of the enemy to escape. The Pawnee scouts charged with the troopers and were free lances, riding everywhere. The herder died fighting in the center of the village, and his pony was killed with him.

"The attack, although made about two* o'clock p.m., was a complete surprise. The troopers were not seen by any of the enemy, except the herder, until they were within fifty yards of the village and charging upon it at a terrific pace. The warriors had no time to seize their arms or secure the ponies. They were completely dazed and bewildered, and fled panic-stricken in every direction. Major Royall and his command joined just as the village was captured and participated in the subsequent operations.

"The village, numbering eighty-four lodges, was rich in everything pertaining to Indian wealth. The Indians were Sioux, Cheyennes, and Arapahoes, under the leadership of Tall Bull, who had been for some years a scourge to the frontier settlements. The bands had intended to separate that morning and abandon the country, as the troops were too strong for them; but they delayed at the Springs, at the suggestion of the medicine-man and against the advice of Tall Bull, and agreed to separate on the morning of the 12th. This delay of twenty-four hours, so fatal to them, gave peace to the western frontiers of Kansas and Nebraska for all time. Tall Bull and sixty* of his warriors were killed and as many were were wounded. A number of women and children were captured and sent to a northern agency. Four hundred and eighteen animals were captured, and ten thousand pounds of dried meat, eighty-four lodges complete, one thousand buffalo-robes, seventy-eight rifles and revolvers, and a large quantity of supplies and camp equipage were destroyed.

"Mrs. Alderdice was killed by a squaw and Mrs. Wiechel was wounded by a warrior at the moment the village was captured. The first was given Christian burial on the field, and the other was taken to Fort Sedgwick, Col., where she recovered. About thirteen hundred dollars were found in the village, and of this amount nine hundred dollars were given to Mrs. Weichel.

"The attack was so impetuous and the surprise so complete that no casualties occurred among the troopers, but a number of horses died of exhaustion. The company commanders who led the charge against the village were recommended for brevet commissions. Complimenatry orders were issued by the colonel of the regiment and the department commander. The division commander telegraphed his congratulations, and the Legislature of Nebraska passed joint resolutions of thanks to Major Carr and the officers and men of the regiment 'for their heroic courage and perseverance in the campaign against hostile Indians on the frontier of the State in July, 1869, driving the enemy from its border and achieving a victory at Summit Springs, Colo., by which the people of the State were freed from the ravages of the merciless savages.'

"This battle ended Indian terrorism in Kansas and Nebraska. The savages had never before received such a stunning blow in any engagement. Wandering bands, notably the Cheyennes in the fall of 1878, have since occasionally created some alarm, but it can be written that for years Kansas and Nebraska have been as secure against Indian outrages as Iowa and Missouri.

"Considered as a complete success, the battle of Summit Springs takes rank with Wichita Village; but in a broader sense it was infinitely greater importance, as it forever secured to the white race the undisputed and unmolested possession of the Republican River and its tributaries."

FROM: *Across the Continent with the Fifth Cavalry* by George F. Price, Nostrand Company, New York, New York, 1883, 14 years after the battle. Price was generally regarded as the regimental historian. His text includes muster rolls and biographies of officers who may have been at Summit Springs.

* Error.

THE NORTH BROTHERS' ACCOUNT

Most likely much data from Luther North rather than Frank, who died in 1886, at age 46.

"General Carr started the command next morning on this Indian trail and followed it westward up the Republican river for two days. They passed several camp-fires, and it was evident that they were gaining on the Indians. Along the trail the print of a woman's shoe was frequently observed, and this was evidence of the fact that they had a white captive with them.

"For this reason General Carr was anxious to press on. In the afternoon of the second day after the discovery of this big trail, the command camped at a vacated Indian camping place where they found numerous fresh antelope heads, showing that the camp had not been abandoned more than twelve or fifteen hours. General Carr concluded to take detachments of the best mounted men from each of the companies with five days rations, and make a forced march until he overtook the Indians, and leave his wagon train to follow as fast as possible.

"Next morning, Sunday, July 11th, the General carried out this plan and got an early start. Major North and ten of his best Pawnee scouts kept in advance, and maintained a sharp look-out for the Indians. The trail led to the north, in the direction of the South Platte river, for a distance of about twenty miles, when Major North suddenly sighted an Indian village from the summit of some sand-hills, near a point that was afterwards named Summit springs. They made a careful survey of the surroundings and saw that it would be impossible for an attack to be made on the village in the direction in which they were going -- which was towards the south -- but that the troops would have to leave the trail and bear off to the east, keeping well out of sight, and then turn again to the north, passing the village and making a semi-circuit to the south and west, and then make the charge upon the village from the north. Major North returned with his scouts to the command, which was eight or nine miles in the rear, and reported the result of his observations, to General Carr, who seemed very much pleased with the information and the prospect of a fight. He at once ordered the cavalry-men to tighten their saddles and prepare for action. The order was obeyed with alacrity, for the men were all eager for a fight, and soon the command was galloping on towards the doomed village. The circuit described by Major North was made, and the command rode within, perhaps, a mile and a half of the village, and could have crept much closer had it not been for a company on the right flank passing over a rise of ground and thus exposing themselves to the view of the village. General Carr was informed of this fact, and being afraid that the company had been observed by the Indians, he at once ordered the bugler to sound the charge, and instantly the stirring notes of the bugle rang out clear and loud, and away dashed the command toward the village. The Indians were lying in camp that day, and their horses were grazing over the prairie at some little distance from the village. They were completely surprised, and before they could realize the situation the cavalrymen had ridden into the village, and the Indians became wholly demoralized. It was a warm, pleasant day, and a great many of the Indians were lounging around in the shade of their tents. They precipitately fled leaving everything behind them, only a few succeeding in reaching their ponies. The soldiers and the Pawnees, as they entered the village, fired volley after volley to the front, to the right and to the left, causing the greatest consternation on every hand. The Sioux* made no resistance to the attack as no opportunity was given them to do so. Many of them fled on foot in every direction, some few escaped on their ponies, while a large number, who were unable to get away by running, dodged into ravines and little pockets and washouts in the nearest hills. All this occupied but a few moments, and as the Sioux* had been scattered, the soldiers, in squads, began hunting them through the nearest ravines.

Major North and his brother, Captain Luther North, with a party of Pawnees and several soldiers, surrounded one of the ravines into which eighteen Sioux warriors and a squaw and a child had fled for safety. One of the warriors, as was afterwards learned, was the noted chief Tall Bull, to whom the squaw and child belonged. He and they were mounted on a beautiful orange-colored horse, with silver mane and tail. Upon reaching the ravine he placed his squaw and child on the inside where he thought they would be safe, and he then returned to the mouth of the ravine and shot his magnificent steed rather than see him fall into the hands of his enemies.

"The mouth of the ravine was very narrow, and the banks were perpendicular, being from fifteen to twenty feet high. The Indians took their butcher knives and cut holes in the banks for their hands and feet, so that they could climb to the top to discharge their guns and shoot their bows and arrows and then drop down again. In this way they kept Major North and his party at bay for some little time. Major North's men, who were stationed about twenty paces from one of the banks of the ravine, kept firing at the Indians as they climbed up on the opposite bank. While this was going on, one of the Indians climbed the bank nearest to the soldiers, and raising his rifle slowly over the top of the bank he laid it down on the ground, and then poking it up sufficiently to take a sight along the barrel of the weapon he fired directly at Major North but missed him. Captain Luther North, at first, surely thought his brother was killed as he had witnessed the movement which had occupied but a moment, so quickly was it done. Major North marked well the spot where the Indian had dropped his head out of sight, being convinced that as soon as the redskin could reload his gun he would make another attempt. The Major dropped down on one knee, and taking a rest on the other, aimed his gun at this particular spot, and waited for the reappearance of the Indian's head. In a few moments he saw the Indian's rifle coming up over the edge of the bank, as it had done before, and soon the Indian raised his head up to take aim. Major North instantly fired, and the Indian dropped without shooting. Major North's bullet had penetrated his forehead, and he fell into the pit a dead man, leaving his rifle, cocked and ready for shooting, on the top of the bank. Later in the day the dead chief, Tall Bull, was found in the ravine, directly under the spot where he had climbed up to fire at Major North. Shortly after the killing of this chief Major North saw another head peeping up at the same spot, and upon closer observation he saw that it was the head of a squaw. She crawled to the top of the bank and pulled her little six-year-old girl after her. None of the soldiers fired at her as she made signs indicating that she wanted to talk to someone. She walked straight up to Major North, and rubbed her hands over him from head to foot as an act of blessing and an appeal for mercy. She then knelt down before him; and, in her sign language, asked him to save her. The Major replied in similar language, telling her to go to the rear out of danger, and remain there until he should call for her, and then she would be safe. She informed him that there were yet seven Indians alive in the ravine. The firing was kept up from the ravine a while, but finally it ceased altogether. Thereupon Major North, and some of his men, cautiously approached the ravine and looked over the bank, and down at the bottom they saw the eighteen warriors lying dead, some on top of others as they had fallen back from the banks. The major and his brother returned to the squaw and taking her and her child across the ravine they joined Company B of the Pawnees, commanded by Captain Cushing, who had, soon after the capture of the village, -- in accordance with General Carr's instructions -- made an active search for the white captives who were supposed to be in the camp. They had succeeded in finding the white women, one of whom had been fatally wounded and the other quite seriously. It appears that while Major North was fighting the Indians in the ravine, Captain Cushing in skirmishing through the village had entered the lodge of Tall Bull, the noted chief, and there found these two wounded women, who were Germans, one being named Mrs. Alderdice, and the other Mrs. Weichel. When the fight commenced Tall Bull, seeing that there was no hope of taking his captives with him, -- whom he had been keeping as his wives -- shot Mrs. Alderdice in the forehead, and then shot Mrs. Weichel. When the Pawnees dashed up to the lodge Mrs. Weichel thought the village had been attacked by Indians hostile to the Sioux, and that she was about to escape from one band only to fall a captive into the hands of another. Therefore, when she discovered Captain Cushing with the Pawnees she manifested the greatest joy imaginable. She was sitting on a mat in the tent, suffering intensely from the wound, but when Captain Cushing stepped up to her she seemed to forget her pain, and grabbing him around the legs she hugged him again and again and wept for joy. She could not speak a word of English and he could not understand what she said. He endeavored, however, by signs and by speaking to her in English, to make her sit still for a little while, and then she would be properly cared for. He finally broke loose from her, and it was at this time that Major North and his brother, with the Sioux* squaw and child, joined the interesting group. Just as they came up the other woman, Mrs. Alderdice, who lay unconscious on the ground and weltering in her blood, drew one or two long breaths and then died.

"The Pawnees then resumed the hunt for Sioux* in the vicinity, and several running fights ensued for some distance beyond the village. After the Sioux had all been driven away from the village, and the fighting was concluded, Mrs. Weichel was taken to the surgeon's tent, where she had her wound dressed, and was otherwise cared for.

"The result of the attack on the village was the killing of fifty-two warriors, and the capture of eighteen squaws and children, and besides there were quite a large number of the Sioux wounded. The soldiers at once rounded up the Indian horses and mules roaming at large and scattered over the prairie, and upon counting them they found that they had captured two hundred and seventy-four horses and one hundred and forty-four mules. The village proved to be a very rich one. The Sioux* had an abundance of everything usually found in an Indian camp, besides a great number of articles which they had obtained from the white settlers whom they had killed on the Saline river. Quite a large amount of gold and silver money and considerably jewelery were also found by the soldiers among the plunder.

"That night the command camped in the captured village; and, at a late hour, the wagon train arrived.

"Mrs. Alderdice, the murdered woman, was buried on the battle field, the burial service being read by one of the officers, who was a religious man, there being no chaplain with the command. General Carr gave the name of Susannah to the place where the battle occurred, that being the Christian name of Mrs. Alderdice, as was learned from Mrs. Weichel. The name was afterwards changed to Summit Springs because there was a fine spring of water on the summit of the sand-hills between the Platte river and Frenchman creek, where nobody would suppose there was any water.

"The next morning all the Indian tepees, lodges, buffalo robes, camp equipage and provisions, including several tons of dried buffalo meat were gathered together in several large piles, and burned, by order of General Carr.

"The command moved down the Platte river the next day, about eight miles, and soon after going into camp Mrs. Weichel was brought into the presence of the Indian prisoners. She at once recognized the squaw who had surrendered herself to Major North, as being the wife of Tall Bull. Mrs. Weichel stated that this squaw, had, on many occasions, whipped and pounded her, and treated her most cruelly and shamefully, during the absence of Tall Bull on hunting expeditions. She explained that the cause of the squaw's cruelty was jealousy, and that during their captivity she and Mrs. Alderdice had never been allowed to meet and talk with each other more than half a dozen times, and she therefore knew but very little concerning the history of the dead woman.

"The Pawnee scouts, who had charge of the prisoners, upon learning of Mrs. Weichel's statement of how badly she had been treated, wanted to kill Tall Bull's squaw then and there, and Major North heard of their intention just in time to prevent it from being carried into execution. However, they said that if she made the slightest attempt to escape, they would kill her on the spot.

"At this camp General Carr issued an order that all the money captured at the village should be turned over to his adjutant, whom he directed to give it to Mrs. Weichel, as she had stated that her father, a short time previous to the massacre, had come over from Germany and that nearly all the gold found in the possession of the Indians had belonged to him.

"Major North collected six hundred dollars in twenty dollar gold pieces from his Pawnee scouts, who gave it up without a murmer, and this money he turned over to the adjutant. About three hundred dollars was collected from the soldiers, and the whole sum of nine hundred dollars was then given to Mrs. Weichel. There was about six hundred dollars more found in the village, but it was concealed by the soldiers.

"The command now proceeded to Fort Sedgwick, at Julesburg, from which point the first news of the fight was telegraphed to military headquarters and all parts of the country.

"The wounded white woman was cared for in the hospital, and shortly after her recovery she married the hospital steward, her husband having been killed by the Indians.

"The Indian prisoners were sent to the Whetstone agency, on the Missouri river, where Spotted Tail and the friendly Sioux were then living, and the captured horses and mules were distributed among the officer, scouts and soldiers."

FROM an unpublished manuscript by Sorrenson, "Quarter of the Century on the Frontier" as told by or from papers of Frank and/or Luther North, Nebraska State Historical Society Archives, first published in E. N. Barr *History of Kansas,* 1908. Frank was commander of the Pawnee scouts. His younger brother, Luther, was twenty-three years old, the same age as Bill

Cody, at Summit Springs. In his later years, Luther North was the source of several conflicting accounts on Summit Springs.

* Error.

THE MAJOR LESTER WALKER ACCOUNT

"In 1869 I was stationed at Fort McPherson, Nebraska. This fort was located 300 miles west of Omaha on the Platte River.

"In June the commander of the Post, General Carr, received orders from the Department Commander, General Augur, to proceed with eight companies on the 5th Cavalry and four companies of the Pawnee Scouts under command of Major North to the Solomon River in Kansas, where two men had been murdered and their wives captured by Indians. Colonel Cody was then chief of scouts, having been appointed by General Sheridan.

"The trail was found soon after the arrival of the troops in the vicinity of the Solomon. The trail was followed to the Republican River in Nebraska and to all the small streams, Red Willow, Medicine, Stinking Water and other creeks and streams until we reached the Platte River between old Fort Sedgwick and Denver.

"Then the trail was lost. No sign of any trail could be seen. General Carr ordered Cody to try and find the trail. He also ordered Major North to send some of his best scouts to locate the trail if possible. Six Pawnee scouts left the command, going down the river. Cody went alone over the hill to the west.

"In about an hour Cody returned to the command with the report that he had found the village, that it was about one half mile long located at some springs. He reported that there was a large band with their families and several hundred mules and ponies. While Cody was reporting to the general the Pawnee scouts returned, informing the General that they had found a trail. General Carr ordered me to take a squadron of Cody* and Captain North's company of Pawnee scouts and see if the trail led to any sizable number of Indians, but left it to me to return if I found the trail to be of no service. General Carr started the balance of the command with Col. Cody as guide. I soon found the trail of the Pawnees to be of no service and returned to the point where I had left the main command and followed General Carr. After marching about five miles I overtook the command. We were now near the point where Cody said we would find the camp.

"The command was halted in a valley and Gen. Carr, Cody and Major North and myself crawled up to the top of the hill overlooking the valley where the Indians were located. We estimated the distance from the top of the hill to the camp to be one mile. This ground had to be covered before we could strike a blow, and this would give the Indians time to mount and give us battle.

"The troops were divided into three columns. Major Maby with one squadron was order to the extreme right and Major Summer and his company and the Pawnee scouts under Major North to the left. I had five companies to charge the center. General Carr rode south west and carried the battle flag until he reached a point, when the charge was ordered. Gen. Carr said to me, 'Now, Major, charge.' I ordered the bugle to sound the charge.

"In going from the hills to the point where the charge was ordered, we went at a fast gallop, regulating the command on the slowest horses. At this time we did not know of swampy ground between us and the Indian village. And General Carr and escort left the column to command the whole field. Between my command the Indians was a marsh formed by the springs and quite a number of my troops foundered in the mire. But we soon crossed over the low ground.

"The Indians had the two women by the hair, trying to pull them onto their ponies and they were resisting. We were so close to them that I feared a stray bullet from my troops might kill the women. At this moment both women were shot by the Indians. One was mortally wounded and died that night. We buried her, wrapped in a blanket, the other was brought to the old Fort Sedgwick on the Union Pacific R.R.* My men killed the two Indians that shot the women. I followed the Indians about three miles beyond the village and captured quite a large number of mules and ponies.

"This band was under Tall Bull, a noted chief. During the engagement Tall Bull was killed and his squaw and children were captured and later send to the Indian Reservation.

"The number of Indians killed was about 150*. The number of soldiers engaged was 450* and 200* Pawnee Scouts.

"Our wagon train consisted of 100 four and six mule teams, with a wagon master for every 20 wagons. Lieut. Hays was Quarter Master and kept his train up with the column while on the march. Several hundred buffalo robes were found in the camp. These were burned with the camp.

"Before going into the charge, the Pawnees stripped themselves of their soldier clothes and put on their war paint. I could not tell a Pawnee scout from the Sioux*.

"This battle took place about 4 o'clock on July 11, 1869 and it must have been a complete surprise to the Indians for they did not have a man on guard. In the charge while crossing the marsh my horse went down and I mounted a horse of one of my men.

"The credit for locating the Indians is to Colonel Cody. He made it possible for the troops to clear the country of these bands of Indians. Quite a number of women and children were captured and later sent to the Indian territory. When Tall Bull was killed, his horse, a fine race horse, was given to Colonel Cody by General Carr.

"After this battle the whole command marched to Fort Sedgwick, and the captured stock was sent to Fort McPherson, Nebraska. General Carr and his officers and men received the thanks of the legislatures of Colorado and Nebraska for clearing the country of Indians."

FROM: The *North Platte Telegraph,* North Platte, Nebraska, Wednesday, 1 March 1967. The account was written by Lester Walker sometime prior to his death in 1916; he was 80 years old. The account was written in longhand, in pencil on ruled tablet paper. Walker was 33 years old at the Battle of Summit Springs.

* Error.

THE J. E. WELCH ACCOUNT

"On the tenth of July we marched sixty-five miles, passing three of their camps. On the eleventh we were on the march before daylight. The trail was hot, the Indians making for the Platte. Every one knew that if they succeeded in crossing the river the game was up. By noon we had marched thirty-five miles, at which time Buffalo Bill, who had been far in advance of the command all day, was seen approaching as fast as his tired horse could come. As soon as he reached the column he called for a fresh horse, and while transferring his saddle told General Carr that he had encountered two bucks who were hunting and that the Indian camp was about twelve miles ahead.

"The general, knowing the bucks who had been run off by Cody would make every effort to reach their camp ahead of us in order to give the alarm, gave the command 'Trot'. Both horses and men seemed to brighten up, and we put real estate behind us at a rapid rate. When within a mile of the hostile camp a halt was called to let the Pawnees unsaddle, as they flatly refused to go into action with saddles on their horses. They began daubing their faces with paint and throwing off their clothing. They were made to retain enough of the latter to enable us to distinguish them from the hostiles. After this short delay we moved forward at a sharp trot, and in a few moments were looking down at 'Tall Bull's' camp in a small valley below us. In a moment the camp was alive with Indians running in every direction.

"General Carr, taking in the situation at a glance, gave utterance to a few words of command, winding up his remarks with the order, given loud and clear and sharp: 'Charge'.

"Every horse leaped forward at the word, and in a twinkling we were among them and the fight was on. It did not last long. There was rapid firing for about five minutes, when all was over except an occasional shot as some fellow would find an Indian who had failed to secure a horse and escape.

"The result of the fight was about as following: no white men killed, four or five horses killed, about one hundred and eighty-eight* dead Indians, forty of whom were squaws and children; one hundred and five* lodges captured, many rifles, five tons of dried buffalo meat baled for winter use, a very ample supply of ammunition, consisting of powder, lead, etc., and a greater number and variety of brass kettles than I ever saw before.

"Of their live stock we captured five hundred and sixty head of ponies and mules.

"To pursue those who had fled was out of the question, our horses being too badly done up. As we charged the camp, we saw a white woman run from among the Indians, one of whom fired at her as she ran. We shouted to her to lie down, which she did, our horses leaping over her without a hoof touching her. She was wounded in her side, but not fatally. Almost at the same moment we saw an Indian seize another white woman by the hair and brain her with a tomahawk. Some of us rode straight for that Indian, and there was not a bone left in his dead carcass that was not broken by a bullet. I dismounted in the midst of the hubbub to see if I could help the woman, but the poor creature was dead. (She had the appearance of being far gone in pregnancy.) I mounted my horse again with a very good stomach for a fight.

"After firing a few shots, I happened to see a Red mounted on a large paint pony making off by himself, and driving four fine mules ahead of him. I gave chase and gained on him rapidly, which he soon perceived, dropping his mules and doing the best he could to get away. But it was no use. 'Sam', my horse, was Kentucky bred, and walked right up on him. When I was within seventy-five or one hundred yards of him he wheeled his horse and fired, the bullet passing through the calf of my leg and into my horse. The Indian threw his gun away and rode at me like a man, discharging arrows as he came. The third arrow split my left ear right up to my head. It was then my turn, and I shot him through the head. This Indian's name was 'Pretty Bear'. He was chief of a band of Cheyennes. The Pawnees knew him and were anxious to secure his scalp. which I was glad to give them as I soon became disgusted with the ghastly trophy. 'Pretty Bear' had on his person the badge of a Royal Arch Mason, with West Springfield, Ill., engraved on it. I sent the badge to the postmaster at Springfield with a statement as to how it came into my possession. 'Pretty Bear' had five or six scalps on the trail of his shield, one of which was that of a woman. The hair was brown, very long, and silken.

"Tall Bull, the Sioux* chief, was killed by Lieutenant Mason, who rode up to him and shot him through the heart with a derringer. After I had taken the scalp of 'Pretty Bear' I found that Sam was shot through the bowels. I unsaddled him and turned him loose to die, but he followed me like a dog and would put his head against me and push, groaning like a person. I was forced to shoot him to end his misery. I had to try two or three times before I could do it. At first to save my life I could not do it. He kept looking at me with his great brown eyes. When I did fire he never knew what hurt him. He was a splendid horse, and could do his mile in 1.57.

"My wounds being slight, I rustled around and soon managed to catch a small mule, which I mounted bareback, intending to scout around a little. I did not carry out my intention, however. The brevet horse ran into the middle of the Indian camp, threw me into a big black mud-hole, my boot was full of blood, my ear had bled all over one side of me, so that when I crawled out of that mud-hole I was just too sweet for anything. By this time the fight was over. A friend of mine, Bill Steele, went with me to the spring that ran into the mud-hole, where he washed me as well as he could, bandaged my leg, sewed my ear together with an awl and some linen thread. He made a good job of it, and I was all right except that my leg was a little sore and stiff.

"After the fight we found we had one hundred and seventeen prisoners*, four squaws, and fifteen children. They were turned over to the Pawnees. The Pawnees did not fight well. They skulked and killed the women and children. I have never seen Indians face the music like white men. We camped where we were that night. Men were coming into camp all night. In fact, they did not reach the scene of action until about ten o'clock next day. They were fellows who had been left along the trail by reason of their horses giving out.

"Our first duty next day was to bury the poor woman they had so foully murdered the day before. Not having a coffin, we wrapped her in a buffalo robe. General Carr read the funeral service and the cavalry sounded the funeral dirge, and as the soft, mournful notes died away many a cheek was wet that had long been a stranger to tears. The other woman was found to be all right with the exception of a wound in the side. She was a German, unable to speak English. Both of the women had been beaten and outraged in every conceivable manner. Their condition was pitiful beyond any power of mine to portray.

"The Indian camp and everything pertaining thereto was destroyed, after which we took up our line of march for Fort Sedgwick, where we arrived in due time without any mishap."

FROM: *Indian Fights and Fighters,* by Cyrus Townsend Brady, published by McClure, Philips & Company, 1904; From letter by Welch to his friend Col. Henry Clark. In a 1971 reprint of the book by the University of Nebraska Press, historian, Dr. James T. King gives his opinion that the account is less than adequate; that Welch was a volunteer, was not closely in tune with Carr's command, and his account has questionable merit.

* Error.

THE HERCULES H. PRICE LETTERS

Price's letters, written 40 years after the battle, have considerable errors and unsubstantiated accounts. His reminiscences are too colorful, however, not to be presented. They are impressions through the eyes of a typical soldier.

He was in Company G, of the 5th Signal Corps, under Lieutenant Adolph Greeley's command. While performing his signal work he relates: "we were in many instances in exposed positions and liable to be cut off by the Indians at any moment. During the night, while signaling, a guard was supplied to each man to hold his horse while using the signal torch, and to guard against surprise."

In describing the chase, Price mentions that the trail they followed had "many moccasin tracks, also lodge pole tracks." He also is the author of the tale about finding a note. He states that they came across a piece of torn dress, then found a note on a scrap of paper pleading, "For God's sake, come and rescue us."

During the Expedition, he became good friends with one of North's Pawnee scouts, and he wrote that "on the march (the scout) would often find and bring me wild plums and gooseberries. It was he who gave me the name of 'Nah-wee-lits-ah-weel' which signifies in their language 'Man who carries a flag'. Our signal party was always invited to join the circle to smoke the tomahawk pipe when we halted to rest the horses and men. It was a handsome pipe, beautifully beaded and the steel was kept as sharp as a razor."

Price seems to have been impressed with the Pawnee. The following is his description of the early morning rendezvous (July 11th) before the battle. "It was in the early dawn of morning, and the groups of Indian scouts on their ponies were wrapped in their blankets in picturesque folds. It was truly a scene for the pencil of an artist. One Indian in particular engaged my attention. I observed him in profile. His nose was Roman, his complexion very dark. He had large black and lustrous eyes and with long ropes of black hair hanging down his back, he was little short of magnificent."

One of Price's comrades, "Lonnie Duke," had been a European soldier. He had been presented the Victoria Cross by Queen Victoria, and the Order of Medjideh by the Sultan of Turkey. He was "trumpeter on the day of the charge of Balaklava (Russian War) and was one of the 600 of Tennyson's poem. The San Francisco Chronicle interviewed him in 1874, and photographed him on his discharge from the army."

An unusual feature of the battle was the use of the sword. Price indicates some men had used recently sharpened sabres against the Indians. Trooper Graham, a bold soldier, rode his horse directly up to a Dog Soldier and "with sabre point, ran it through, killing him instantly."

During the battle, Price was ordered to report to Carr. "The General ordered me to replace the carbine in the carbine boot and advance pistol, for he said he wanted me as one of his bodyguards and also to transmit by flag messages across the scene of action to some troops engaged with a body of Indians. An interesting spectacle I observed upon my way to report to General Carr was a line of dogs belonging to our men on the top of the bluff over-looking the camp. They were turning to one another and watching intently, and seemed fully conscious of the conflict going on, though safe from harm." His own dog, a small black and tan terrier which he brought from Atlanta, Georgia, was with the pack on the bluff.

When there was a lull in the fighting, several wounded warriors and squaws were discovered in a flat canyon southwest of the creek. A soldier attempted to give a wounded squaw some water, but "she dashed at him with a knife and but for his brother officer quickly pulling him back he would have been severely stabbed."

The trumpeter of Company G, Henry Voss, a native of Holland, interpreted for Doctor Tesson, General Carr, and Maria Weichell. Voss later joined the 7th Cavalry and "was probably massacred on the Big Horn," with Custer.

Susanna Alderdice was "buried with military honors"... "three volleys were fired" over her grave which "was at the upper right hand side of the creek, ascending the hillside." In honor of her the "springs on the mesa lands" were named "Susanna Springs" (afterward changed back to Summit Springs).

The spoils of the battle picked up by Price included: "Tall Bull's squaw's shirt, an article beautifully beaded in diamond patterns, with thick buckskin fringe at the hips intermingled with tin bells....two buffalo robes and several pair of moccasins of the Cheyenne pattern. The shirt I sold for $5.00." He also found a small Bible and ledger book. The Bible was fastened with clasps and a "thin brass marker was clasped to two sheets in the Old Testament at the passage stating: 'Ye shall go into the land of the Phillistines and ye shall utterly destroy them,' and surely enough, we did almost destroy the red scourges of the plains."

Also found were notes "written by the son of a New York merchant who was a captive." His fate was not known... "doubtless it was a death in some horrible form since Indians seldom carry male captives along."

On a gaily painted pack horse, were found "wads of greenbacks and gold and silver coins (which) were indiscriminately bundled together... some soldiers got considerable money... this was common talk long after the battle. A deserter communicated the statement to his comrades that '$38,000 was hauled in by him'."

The horse captured by Buffalo Bill was a well bred "iron grey." Among the other captured animals were "a number of fine American horses," and a large amount of "fat Indian ponies." Four sets of silver mounted harnesses for "eight cream colored ponies with white manes and tails were sent East as a present to someone high in government affairs."

Significant errors in the Hercules Price letters include: the date when the Republican River Campaign began, soldiers being killed during the chase, a battle starting prior to reaching the Indian camp at Summit Springs, the battle starting at noon, and his recollection of almost three times as many Indian lodges as existed. In agreement with Cody, however, he wrote that "General Carr gave the order to blow the charge which was eventually done by L. Hayes, the quartermaster, the bugler being for some reason temporarily incapacitated."

REFERENCES: *History of Lincoln County, Kansas,* Elizabeth Barr, 1908, *Lincoln Sentinel,* "Historical Sketches", J. J. Peate, 1932, and *Pioneer History of Kansas,* Adolph Roenigk, 1933.

THE ELI ZEIGLER ACCOUNT OF SPILLMAN CREEK

"John Alverson, my brother-in-law, took his team which we loaded with corn and oats to plant, also provisions for two weeks for ourselves and horses, expecting to be away that length of time. We started from father's place Sunday, May 30, 1869, and got up to Thomas Alderdice's at noon and ate our dinner there. Thomas Alderdice, I think was in Salina. I do not remember of talking with any man in that settlement. Report said that the Indians had been on the Solomon river a few days before, but they had been driven off by a company of soldiers. My sister, Mrs. Alderdice, mentioned that and told me to keep a sharp lookout. After eating dinner with my sister, I bade her good bye -- little thinking that she would be in the hands of the Indians before sundown, her children killed or wounded, and that I would never see her again. After going a short distance I saw a man on horse-back up toward the head of Lost creek, riding fast toward the west. John thought he looked like an Indian spy, but I thought it was some one looking for cattle. We kept close watch on him to see where he was going, but he gained so rapidly on us that we could soon see him only on the highest hills. He was still riding at full speed the last we saw of him on the hill east of Trail creek, and the course he was taking he would cross Trail creek about where the wagon road crossed, or a little above. We kept on going on across Trail creek when John made the remark that he did not like the appearance of things. After we left this creek going towards Spillman creek, as we approached the highest ground we could look up the bottom on the south of Spillman and there we saw a party of horsemen quite a way up the creek, and coming down the bottom quite rapidly. We stopped a moment to look at them, and John thought they were Indians, and that was their spy who went ahead of us, but I thought that they were soldiers, returning from the Solomon river. They deceived me the way they rode, riding like a company of soldiers in uniform line, and coming at a fast gallop. The sun glistened on their guns so plain that I still thought they were soldiers, but John would not have it that way, but said they were Indians, and I had about made up my mind that they were. They were getting by this time about opposite us and we had tried to count them several times. As near as we could make out there were between 45 and 60 of them. At this time they were still south of Spillman creek and a little above the Dane settlement.

"We had made up our minds that there was no way of avoiding an attack. Just then they stopped, and we stopped a moment, the distance between us being about one-half mile. Then they all started for us on the run, except ten or fifteen who went down the creek toward the Dane Settlement. There was a knoll just north of us, and I thought best to get on that and fight there, thinking that we would have time to unhitch the horses and tie them to the wagon before they got to us. So we drove to the knoll. I jumped out to unhook the horses, but John thought it would not do to stop there, there being so many Indians he thought best for us to get to the creek. I jumped back into the wagon and we started toward Trail creek, going in a northeasterly direction to the nearest point. We came to the creek about half a mile above the crossing. As we were not very well armed we talked the matter over while going to the creek. I having a needle gun and about forty rounds of cartridges and John an old muzzle loader, we concluded that I would do the shooting and John would hold the load in his gun as a reserve shot.

"When we got to the creek the Indians were close behind us. I looked across the creek and thought there was a little bank on the other side that would protect us some. So, I drove across, but John misunderstood me and jumped out into the creek and I drove up the bank. John ran along under the bank on the side I was on; the Indians were coming across the creek within a few yards of us, shooting and yelling. John was calling for me to get out of the wagon, when I got to that little bank, I stopped the horses seeing nothing more could be done to save the team and that we must defend ourselves. I dropped the lines, grabbed my gun and jumped out on the off side of the wagon. Reaching in the box for my cartridges, I could get only the box, about 20 rounds. While I was getting the cartridges the Indians were close all around. One of them rode up and picked up the lines just as I had laid them down and he held the horses. I thought sure I'll put a hole through you, but before I could get my gun around he jumped off his pony down beside the wagon, and still held the horses. The Indians were shooting all this time. John was calling for me to get under the bank. Just then another Indian darted up right close to the wagon and I thought I would get him sure, but before I could cover him with my gun he jumped his pony on the opposite side of the wagon, so I could not get him.

"John was still begging me to jump over the bank and I had about made up my mind to. As I stepped out from the wagon I looked toward the rear and behind the wagon and saw three Indians standing about four rods away, having me covered with their guns. I had no time for a shot, so made a spring for the creek bank; my foot slipped and I fell just as they fired. I think they over shot me. I also think that the slip is what saved me. I kept going on my hands and feet over the bank. As they were pouring the shots right at us at short range we saw a log lying up the bank a little below us, we ran to that, thinking it would protect us on the side. We expected a good, long, hard fight, but as we ran to the log and jumped over, getting ourselves into position, the Indians, I guess saw that we were going to try to protect ourselves. They kept back on the bank out of our sight, and drove the team away just after we got behind the log, and the Indians quit shooting at us. Then we could hear shooting down the creek near the Dane settlement, when John said, 'My God! They are fighting down at the Dane settlement.' This firing did not last long, and we thought it was the small band that went down that way and that there would be enough of the whites there to stand them off and get in position by the time the band that had attacked us concluded to withdraw and go down and re-enforce their comrades.

"We kept waiting behind the log for some time, expecting the Indians were going to slip upon us in some way around the creek banks, and we were prepared for them. If John had had a good repeating gun when we were under the creek bank, he had plenty of opportunity to make a few GOOD Indians, but did not dare to shoot that one load out while by himself. We lay there by the log quite a little time in readiness. We did not hear any more of the Indians, and did not see anything of them. I then crawled up the creek bank to take a look. Away down on the east side of Spillman creek I saw two or three horsemen, which I thought were Indians. Concluding that the Indians had left us, we decided to try and go down to the Dane settlement.

"We expected the Indians to lie in ambush for us along the creek, therefore we worked our way slowly and carefully, every little ways going up the bank to see if we could see anything of the Indians.

"Seeing no signs of foes, we would keep on going, and we passed the Dane settlement before sundown. We would go up the bank watching closely and listen, expecting to hear somebody or see where the Indians had been. We knew there were settlers near there, but did not know where their house was located. Not seeing their house, we passed on. Continuing our journey along the creek slowly and cautiously, we thought that the Indians had not gone farther than the Dane settlement, and that they had probably gone back, as we could not see or hear anything of them. It was now growing dark, and we thought best to keep on the safe side and keep close to the creek, so in case they had gone farther down, and were on their way back, we would meet them in a place where we would have the advantage.

"We followed Spillman creek down to its mouth, then down the Saline. I do not know what time of the night it was, but it was several hours after dark. We had not seen or heard anything since leaving our log on Trail creek, and concluded that the Indians had not passed down Spillman creek farther than the Dane settlement, that they had not been in the settlement on the Saline river. We were now about a mile west of where the depot now stands at Lincoln, when the stillness of the night was broken by a loud war song northeast of us and down the valley. John said, 'My God, Eli, they have been down to the settlement.' We heard more singing farther down and nearer the river. I said, 'Yes, John, I fear it is a big party, and think it is a different party from the one we ran into.'

"I thought this was a larger party that had come down the Saline, probably dividing on Wolf creek. We could tell they were moving up the Saline bottom by the noise they made, sounding like a large party or else they were scattered out. They did not seem to be coming very fast, some were singing and others were talking loudly.

"We got to the bank of the river, one of the bends which points to the north. When they got opposite and close enough we were going to fire towards them, we were going to fire together and I was to keep on firing while John loaded again. If the Indians came toward us, we would cross the river, but we did not think they would attack us in the dark. By this time they were pretty well north of us, but quite aways out off of the bottom. All at once they commenced hallooing and fired several shots. As the last shots were fired, we heard a woman scream one loud piercing scream, a scream more of horror than of agony, then all was still.

"We could not imagine who it was that had fallen into

the hands of the Indians, there being no one living in the direction from which the scream came. We almost held our breath while we listened, wondering what the Indians were doing, and which way they were moving, waiting and listening, and waiting for the sound of their ponies, walking through the grass, a voice, a sigh, or a moan, but not a sound reached us. In a few moments which seemed hours to us, we heard them east of us down the river. John thought it best to get down the river ahead of them, but I could not see how we could head them off if we were to follow them directly down the river. Being sure that they were now down in the settlement, we crossed the river in the direction of Bullfoot creek, by so doing we could travel faster and perhaps get there ahead of the Indians.

"Starting a little east of south, when we got on high ground between the Saline and Bullfoot we saw several fire signal arrows shooting up into the sky, from up Bullfoot west and south of us. Thinking then that there must be three bands of Indians, one coming down the Spillman, one down the Saline, and the other down the Bullfoot, we feared that when daylight came, all we could see would be Indians, Indians everywhere.

"Wishing to get ahead of them we turned a little east, getting to the creek as soon as possible; when, thinking we were below them we hurried down the creek as fast as we could under the circumstances, keeping our guns ready to fire at the first sight of a moving Indian.

"We had made up our minds that if we ran into them again we were going to do some good shooting at the first one we saw, without waiting for good one or fat one. Traveling on down the creek, dawn was fast approaching, we were still hugging the creek for protection in case of need. We had not heard a sound or seen a signal light since those mentioned.

"About sun up or a little after, we were near Fred Erhardt's place, where we found a company of United States cavalry in camp. We reported to the captain what we had seen -- told him what we had heard in the night, out on the Saline river bottom, and of the fire arrows we had seen just a little above on Bullfoot. I begged him to saddle up at once -- to furnish me a horse and I would lead them right to the Indians camp, where I thought we could catch them if we moved at once and moved quickly. He replied, 'I cannot move any farther until I get orders to do so. The Indians were in the settlement over the river yesterday afternoon, but I do not know how much damage they have done.' He had sent a dispatch to Fort Harker for orders and would wait there until he received an answer. We were disgusted with his reply, drank a cup of coffee, ate a hard tack and started on home, keeping on the south side of the river, and just before noon got home.

"I got my pony, intending to go back up the river, but as we had told the folks the story, they would not let me go until next day, when I went up. But the dead, except one, had been found, and all the wounded. My sister, Mrs. Alderdice, had been captured.

"The next day, A. M. Campbell and some others came up from Salina, with whom I went up on Spillman creek to look the ground over, and to see if we could find Petersen, the missing Dane. Finding his body, we dug his grave where he fell, on the south side of Spillman. We also saw the graves of the others that the Indians had killed. They were buried by the party that were there May 31, 1869. We also saw where the Indians had been at the dug-out, where the Danes lived. I knew now that we were wrong in thinking there were three parties or bands of Indians. There was but one band; we were following this party around, that made us think we were seeing different bands.

"The shooting on the Saline river was where the two men, T. Meigerhoff and G. Weichell were killed, and Mrs. Weichell was captured. They must have crossed the river after killing these two men near us, and went over to Bullfoot, and not down the river as we thought at that time, but we following them over caused us to think them another party."

FROM: *Lincoln Sentinel,* October 18, 1909; From a letter by Eli Zeigler to his friend J. J. Peate in 1909, forty years after the indian raid. Zeigler was 18 years old in 1869, and was the younger brother of Susan Alderdice. He was one of the Forsythe's Scouts at the famous Beecher Island battle.

THE WASHINGTON SMITH ACCOUNT OF SPILLMAN CREEK

"On the last day of May 1869, as Eli Zeigler and John Alverson were going up the Spillman Creek to visit a claim, they saw what appeared to be a body of soldiers, clad in blue blouses and marching four abreast over the hills. On nearing, the block house, Zeigler and Alverson found them to be Indians, riding toward them with great speed. Zeigler and his friend then turned about and drove to the nearest timber and threw themselves behind the banks of the stream. They worked their way down the stream to a narrow place, sheltered by deep banks. Here they concealed themselves till late at night when they made their retreat to the settlement. The Indians attacked a settlement of Danes near the mouth of Trail Creek killing Mr. Lauritzen and his wife and left them lying side by side on the ground. They next met young Peterson, who was out staking off a place for a garden with a hatchet. They killed him and hacked his face with the hatchet. It was Sunday, and a beautiful day. All nature was in its loveliest mood, the fields were in bloom. Two friends, Wetzell* and Mayerschoff* and the young wife of the former, were visiting the Danes. They had gone out this beautiful day to walk over their claim. It was about three o'clock in the evening. The men were around when the Indians came in sight. They fought their way down the valley, keeping the Indians off with their guns. When they reached a point about a mile and a half west of Lincoln Center their ammunition gave out. Here they were killed and the woman captured. It is pleasing to note that these men, true to the instincts of manhood, kept this woman with them as long as their powder and ball held out and gave her up only with their lives. These men were natives of Sleswick, Prussia. Their bones now repose in the valley about a mile and a half west of Lincoln Center. They had been in the United States but a few months.

"On this same Sunday evening, Mrs. Olderdise* was visiting Mrs. Kine. They were in a house a mile and a half west of Lincoln Center, near the river. When the Indians came in sight, Mrs. Kine, with one child, and Mrs. Olderdise, with four children, started down the river to a place of security. In crossing a strip of prairie near Nicholas Whalen's, two Indians were seen approaching with great speed. When the Indians were within a few rods, Mrs. Kine started for the river to cross; said Mrs. Olderdise, 'Don't Leave Me.' Mrs. Kine replied,

"'I can do you no good -- I must take care of myself.' The river was up but Mrs. Kine rushed in and crossed with the child in her arms, the water reaching to her shoulders. She followed around the bank and took shelter under the lay of a fallen tree that overhung the river. When the Indians came up, Mrs. Olderdise, overcome with terror and fright, sat down on the ground. The Indians then shot the three little boys. Two of them they killed outright; the other they shot in the back and left for dead. They then put Mrs. Olderdise on a pony, the child in her arms, and took her off. It is said they camped that night on Bull Foot Creek, and there they cooked the child to death. On this Sunday evening, two boys, Harrison Strange, fourteen years of age, and a boy named Schmutz, thirteen years old, were on the hill, about a thousand yards south of Lincoln Center, digging a root resembling a turnip, with a pick. Two Indians was seen riding up, the one a stout middle-aged Indian; the other a youth sixteen or seventeen years old. The young Indian carried a club, made of mountain pine. At sight of these, the boys started to run, but the old Indian called out, 'good Pawnee' which the boys understood to mean friendly Indian. The boys stopped. The old Indian then rode up and tapped each of the boys gently with a spear. He then galloped off after some loose horses. By this time the young Indian had rode very close to the boys. He then raised himself high in the stirrups, with the club in both hands. Young Strange saw the blow coming and with the words, 'Oh Lord' half expressed, he fell and died almost instantly, his skull having been broken in near the crown. The club broke and was left lying on the ground near by. For these facts I am indebted to young Schmutz. Young Schmutz then ran and dodged. The Indian shot at him several times, one arrow striking him in the side. He pulled the shaft of this out but left the barb buried in his side. When the Indian saw the brothers of young Strange coming to their relief he galloped off. Schmutz was taken to Fort Harker and placed in the hospital where he lingered ten weeks and died. The next day when the settlers went out to gather up the dead, they found one of Mrs. Olderdise's boys still alive, an arrow sticking in his back. They brought him to the house of William Hendrickson, whereby, the sturdy hand of Phil Lance, with a large pair of bullet moulds, the arrow was drawn out and that boy is now the only son of that family left to tell the tale.

"It seems Mrs. Wetzell and Mrs. Olderdise were kept together during their captivity. They tried to lay plans to make their escape, but the one knew nothing of German, the other little of English, and it was hard to talk together. In the summer, Col. Carr stationed on the Platte river, heard there were some captives among the Indians on the frontier. He sent out a company of soldiers to rescue the women, but when the assault was made, the Indians, according to custom, shot the captives. Mrs. Olderdise was killed at the time. Mrs. Wetzell received a glancing shot the ball striking a rib, from which she recovered. She afterward came into the settlements. The soldier who first reached her in the rescue was one whose time had almost expired and Mrs. Wetzel afterward became his wife. She had a large amount of clothing; and many golden ornaments. She had 45 dresses mostly of silk. The gold watch she had on her person at the time she was captured she kept concelaed from the Indians and brought in with her after the rescue. She was quite handsome and about twenty years of age. Mrs. Olderdise was about twenty-eight years of age; of an amiable disposition and endowed with all the delicacy of her sex. She must have endured her captivity in great sorrow."

FROM: *Saline Valley Register,* July 5, 1876 and later reprinted in *Lincoln Republican,* February 3, 1886.

The Honorable Washington Smith was one of the early settlers, and in 1870, was appointed, by the governor, as one of the three official commissioners to organize Lincoln county, Kansas.

* Error.

CHAPTER 9

STORIES BY INDIANS

THE GEORGE BENT STORY

George Bent was the half-breed son of Bents' Fort co-founder, William Bent, and Owl Woman, a Cheyenne. He was wounded at the Sand Creek Massacre in 1864.

"The Dog Soldiers and these two Sioux villages, under Whistler and Two Strikes, now decided to go north and join the Northern Cheyennes and Sioux under Red Cloud. They had no trouble in distancing Carr's outfit, but when they reached the South Platte the river was so high that they were compelled to lie in camp waiting for the flood to subside. Tall Bull sent scouts to the south, in which direction the Indians had their last fight with Carr, but no scouts were sent to the east, as they did not expect any troops from that direction. Pawnee scouts came up on two Cheyenne men and one old woman who were following the village and they killed the two men. The Pawnees told the Cheyennes later that the woman refused to be captured and they were compelled to kill her also. These scouts told Carr which way the trail went.

"Tall Bull was anxious to cross the Platte rivers (north and south forks) and get up into the Black Hills country. He sent Two Crows and five other Cheyennes on ahead to try the South Platte and find a place where it might be forded. This party crossed the South Platte and found the river so high in some places that the water ran over their horses backs. Then they found a place where it was not so high and marked it with sticks. It was evening when they returned to the village and reported to Tall Bull. There was a great deal of excitement in the camp at this time, as a war party of Sioux had come in and reported troops following the trail. Nevertheless Tall Bull sent criers through the camp to announce that they would camp where they were for two days; then they would cross over and camp in the high bluffs near the square butte, known to the whites as Court House Rock, where they could watch for soldiers and could not be surprised. Many of the Sioux, however, insisted on crossing the river that evening. But the Cheyennes went into camp at this place, called by the whites Summit Springs. This is at the base of Freemont Butte or White Butte, and here heads a little stream called White Butte Creek. The Cheyennes say it was poor judgment for Tall Bull to insist on going into camp instead of crossing the South Platte that evening and this error was the cause of the village being surprised next day.

"The Cheyennes agree that the Pawnees and soldiers took them completely by surprise next day (July 11, 1869). The day was a misty one, "smoky" the Indians say. They had been burning the grass to destroy their trail; they say everything looked indistinct. Brave Bear and Two Crows say they were eating the mid-day meal when Carr attacked them. Some of the Indians were lounging on a little hill, but most all were eating. Little Hawk, riding some distance from the camp, first discovered the troops. But he had a slow horse and the Pawnee scouts beat him to the camp. The day being so smoky his signals were not seen. He joined some of the fugitives from the village and got away with them. The Pawnee scouts were in the lead in the charge on the camp, shooting and yelling. Most of the horses were herded close to the camp, and many were tied near the lodges. At the first sound of firing all ran to catch horses before they stampeded. Those with horses in camp quickly mounted the women and children, while the men got ready to fight. Brave Bear and Two Crows ran out of their lodge toward the horses just in time to see all of Tall Bull's own herd stampede. As they ran they heard Tall Bull call in a loud voice, 'All of you that are on foot and cannot get away follow me.' A number of people ran with Tall Bull and his two wives to a little ravine with sharp high banks. By this time the troops were all around, except on the south side of the camp, and the excitement was terrifying. Horses were stampeding in all directions, the Pawnees and soldiers yelling and shooting, women and children screaming with fright, Cheyenne and Sioux men shouting orders to the women and fighting off the attackers. Many people, mounted and on foot, streamed out to the south and scattered over the prairie in little groups, the men fighting off the pursuing Pawnees. Tall Bull's party in the ravine helped divert the soldiers and scouts from the fleeing Indians. The Pawnees, the Cheyennes say, did most of the killing and also captured the greater part of the pony herd. Two Crows ran across the prairie with a party of Cheyennes and Sioux, who covered the flight of a number of Cheyenne and Sioux women and children. Some were mounted, many on foot, and they were strung along the open prairie. The Pawnees followed, shooting and killing, but their horses seemed very tired after their long run up the hill to the Indian camp. Fighting in the rear of these women and children were Kills Many Bulls, Two Crows, and Lone Bear, the latter mounted, the other two on foot. Lone Bear was very brave, Two Crows says, charging again and again into the party of Pawnees chasing them, thus covering the flight of Two Crows and Kills Many Bulls as well as the women and children they were protecting. These three kept turning and fighting off the Pawnees; men in other groups did the same. Once Lone Bear charged right in among the Pawnees and went down fighting like a wild animal. Other Cheyennes say Two Crows was very brave, though he speaks sadly of running away and leaving so many Cheyenne and Sioux women and children to be killed by the Pawnees. After killing Lone Bear, Two Crows says, the Pawnees seemed to have stopped chasing the people. Two Crows had been badly kicked in the shins by a Pawnee horse he was trying to catch. In some way this horse got away from its rider and ran past Two Crows.

"Tall Bull, the Dog Soldier chief, had three wives. One of those he put on a horse when the shooting started and she got away with a daughter of the first wife. The other two wives, the youngest and the eldest, went with Tall Bull to the ravine. In the fighting here the youngest was killed and the other was captured. Powder Face, an old chief, and his Sioux wife went with Tall Bull; also the son of Powder Face, Black Moon, who had been badly wounded some days before and was still very weak. Big Gip and his wife also ran with this party to the ravine. A young Dog Soldier, named Wolf with Plenty of Hair, was very brave and staked himself out with a dog rope at the head of the ravine. It was the custom for the Dog Soldier wearing a dog rope to pin himself down in running fights or when a party was taken by surprise as in this case. The fighting was so hot around the ravine that no one had time to pull the picket pin for Wolf with Plenty of Hair, and after the fight was over he was found where he had staked himself out. The Cheyennes in the ravine put up a desperate fight. Bill Cody and Frank North claim they killed Tall Bull, but the Pawnees say no one knows who killed him, as they were all shooting at him. White Buffalo Woman, wife of Tall Bull and sister of Good Bear, was allowed to come out of the ravine and surrender. She is still living at Tongue River Reservation. The rest of the Cheyennes were killed in the ravine.

"This was one of the severest blows struck against the Dog Soldiers. The troops captured most of the horses and mules and burned and destroyed the camp. The Cheyennes say the surprise was so complete that they wonder why more people were not killed and give the Pawnees the credit for the damage that was done. The names of the Cheyenne men killed were Tall Bull, Black Moon (named after a total eclipse of the moon), Wolf with Plenty of Hair, Powder Face, White Rock, and Lone Bear. A large number of women and children were killed. Of the Sioux we do not know how many were killed. Brave Bear and Yellow Nose were with a party that remained hiding and a month later crossed the Platte and joined the Indians in the north. Both these men married women up there. Yellow Nose did not come south again until Dull Knife's band came down in 1877. Those that went north spent one winter there and then the majority came south again and joined the Southern Cheyennes. Most of the Dog Soldiers, however, straggled south and joined the Southern Cheyennes on the South Fork of the Canadian, staying with the Southern Cheyennes from that time on. I was living near Camp Supply at this time with the Southern Cheyennes."

FROM: *Life of George Bent: Written by His Letters,* by George E. Hyde.

THE CHEYENNE INDIANS' STORY

As told to and reported by George Bird Grinell. Grinnell spent many years among the Cheyenne tribes in the late 1800's.

"So far as known, the first man who saw the troops was Little Hawk, but he was far away from the camp hunting antelope, and was riding a slow horse and could not get to the camp in time to warn the Indians. In fact, the troops reached the village before he could do so, and when he met a number of escaping Cheyennes, he joined them.

"Two Crows was sitting in the lodge talking when he heard someone outside exclaim: 'People are coming.' He paid no attention to the call, but continued his conversation, and presently, without any warning, shooting began to sound close to the camp. All rushed out of the lodge, and saw the Pawnees charging up and down on the near-by hillside and firing into the camp. At first some of the people thought that these Indians were the advance messengers of a Sioux war party that had been out and were returning with scalps, but in a moment or two the soldiers began to pour over the hill. Many of the

Indians had their horses tied up in camp, and in a few moments a number of them had mounted. These took women and children on behind them and started to turn away. The troops appeared on the east side of the village, and on the west side, and presently began to come over the hill from the north. Only the south side was open for the Cheyennes to get away. Meantime there was the confusion that always exists in a surprise attack on an Indian village. Horses were running in every direction; people were trying to catch their horses and were springing on their backs, and many others were running away on foot, some toward the south and others to hiding places in the bluffs.

"Two Crows started on foot, running as hard as he could. As he started, he picked up a rope, a bridle, a pistol, and his medicine war club, which he afterward threw away. As he ran he heard hoofbeats behind him, and looking back, saw coming a herd of loose horses, followed by a Cheyenne, named Plenty of Bull Meat. Two Crows called to him saying: 'Turn the horses toward me,' and as they came up to him, Two Crows saw in the lead a fine black horse belonging to Tall Bull, which he knew as a good and gentle horse. As it ran by him, Two Crows ran fast by its side and made a cast with his rope, which by good luck fell over the horse's head. he had just time to slip the bridle on the horse when close behind came a party of charging Pawnees. By this time two more Cheyennes had joined them.

"Presently they overtook four women riding double, on two horses, and an old man, and immediately behind them were five Pawnees shooting at them. The Pawnee horses were tired out, and they could barely gallop. The old man with these women called out: 'Young men, turn about and come behind these women and whip up their horses and help them to get along.' Two Crows and Plenty of Bull Meat turned and rode behind the women and whipped up their horses, which then ran much faster. The women were so frightened that they seemed not to have thought of urging their horses forward.

"They drove the women forward, and with them the old man. He had a gun, which he did not use, expecting if his horse gave out to get off and fight on foot. Presently they overtook an old woman on foot leading a horse. When they overtook this woman, they recognized her as a very old woman who ordinarily wore the old-fashioned Sŭh'tai woman's dress. They tried to help her on her horse, but they could not do it, and the Pawnees were so close behind them that they did not dare to dismount to lift her. For a little while they tried to fight for her, but when the Pawnees got quite close, they left her and rode on. A little farther along they came upon two Sioux women running on foot, but they were obliged to go on, and the Pawnees killed them.

"Still farther along they came to a Cheyenne woman with two little children, a boy and a girl, running hard, and there they did a bad thing. They stopped and fought for a time, trying to turn the Pawnees, but could do nothing, and rode on, and the Pawnees killed the three. They ought at least to have picked up the little children and carried them away with them and saved them.

"They went on farther, but after this they saw no people on foot. An old Sioux woman's horse fell with her, and she was thrown off and killed by the Pawnees.

"At this time about twenty-five or thirty more Pawnees came up, and a little later Two Crows and Plenty of Bull Meat, Lone Bear and Pile of Bones, who had good horses and were fixed for fighting, saw down below them a woman on a horse going very slowly. Lone Bear called out to the others: 'Now, we must stop here and fight for this woman. You two must do your best. Go down there and help her. We will stay behind and fight these people off.'

"Three Pawnees who had been following the woman were quite close to her, shooting at her. Two Crows and Plenty of Bull Meat rode down to her and whipped her horse and turned it up into the hills, while the three Pawnees rode back toward their fellows. Then Two Crows and Plenty of Bull Meat rode back toward Lone Bear, but before they got to him, the Pawnees had shot him and Pile of Bones, and they had fallen off their horses. The Pawnees had dismounted and were scalping the two men. They were also throwing up into the air the war bonnets that the men had worn. The Pawnees did not attempt to follow Two Crows and Plenty of Bull Meat. These two said: 'It is useless for us to stay here any longer.' and they rode away as fast as they could. They were riding off when on a sudden they met Bad Heart with six other men, and told him what had happened to Lone Bear and Pile of Bones; that they were lying over there where they could see the Pawnees standing.

"Bad Heart said to them: 'Come on, now; let us ride back and see our friends.' The nine men started toward the Pawnees, who by this time had turned and were riding back to the troops. When the Cheyennes got near the Pawnees, they charged them, but the Pawnees' horses were exhausted and could do no more than walk, and presently two of the Pawnees jumped off their horses and started to run. Two Crows tried to ride around the abandoned ponies and drive them off, but one of them kicked up behind and struck him in the shin and kicked his horse in the neck. The Cheyennes rode up to where Lone Bear and Pile of Bones were lying and saw that they had been scalped and cut to pieces.

"Red Cherries, a Northern Cheyenne, was in the camp with his wife and his little baby. Some Cheyennes who had been to war in the south and had captured a lot of mules had come to the camp and told them that soldiers were on their trail, and that with the soldiers were some Pawnees. After two or three moves, when they had camped at Summit Springs, Red Cherries said to his wife: 'We will do well to go north again. These people seem to be dodging about from place to place all the time.' He and his wife had saddled up and started, but met the approaching soldiers and soon after the camp was attacked. The young people, both Sioux and Cheyennes, left the camp and ran away over the prairie, but the old people ran to a deep ravine to hide there. Among them were Tall

Bull, the chief, Black Sun, and Heavy Furred Wolf. Black Sun had been wounded through the body in a fight, but was now up and able to be about. Red Cherries went to the outer edge of the camp, and stopped there and dismounted and turned his saddle horse loose. The Pawnees were already in the camp. A number of young men who rode by him asked him to get on behind them and escape, but to each one he said: 'No, my friend, I shall stop here in this camp.' It was a pretty hard place, for Pawnees and soldiers charged through the camp, following the people. Red Cherries walked around the edge of the camp, and the bullets struck all about him, close to his body. Presently Tall Sioux rode up to him and said: 'Jump on behind me and come away; take pity on your little baby; do not leave it fatherless.'

"'No, my friend,' said Red Cherries, 'I shall stay here.'

"When Tall Sioux received this answer, he rode off. The soldiers were in line on two sides of the camp shooting. Presently Tall Sioux again rode up to him and said: 'Friend, take pity on your wife and child; listen to what I say.'

"As Tall Sioux rode up to him, it seemed that all the guns went off at once, opening and firing. The sound was continual.

"Then Red Cherries said: 'My friend, you have come for me twice and I will listen to you.' He jumped on behind his friend, and they rode off over the hill.

"After they had got beyond the ridge, they stopped, and fought and then retreated, and presently the firing stopped. A little later from far off in the distance they saw five Pawnees come in sight over the hill. The two Cheyennes supposed that these Pawnees were alone and charged down on them, when suddenly coming over the hill were seen more Pawnees and a line of soldiers... All of the camp that was left later crossed the Platte, and did not stop traveling until they reached the Sioux camp on White River. (They crossed the Platte August 7 -- a month after the fight.)"

FROM: *The Fighting Cheyennes,* by George Bird Grinnell.

BUFFALO HERD, 1870
Courtesy: Kansas State Historical Society
Topeka, Kansas

The mainstay for the nomadic Indians way of life, the buffalo (bison) was king of the central plains until the arrival of the white man. The four great Western herds from North to South, were: Northern (Montana), Republican (north of South Platte River), Arkansas (Colorado and Kansas), and Texas (south of Arkansas River). In the late 1860's, the western herds were still so large they interfered with railroad and overland travel. It was not unusual for a herd to delay a train for hours. Herds were described as one mass several miles in each direction. The carnage on southern plains by white hunters reached its peak in 1873, with a million hides being shipped east. By the close of the hunting season of 1875, the herd south of the Platte was basically exterminated. The northern herd was finished off in 1883.

DRYING MEAT, INDIAN VILLAGE
Courtesy: Kansas State Historical Society, Topeka, Kansas.

CAMP OF SOUTHERN CHEYENNE, 1880
Courtesy: Nebraska State Historical Society, Lincoln, Nebraska

LODGE OF CHEYENNE CHIEF WHIRLWIND
Courtesy: Nebraska State Historical Society, Lincoln, Nebraska.

SITTING BULL, SIOUX CHIEF
Courtesy: Cody Ranch, North Platte, Nebraska.

WHITE HORSE, CHEYENNE DOG SOLDIER CHIEF
Courtesy: Smithsonian Institution, Washington, D.C.

PAWNEE KILLER, SIOUX CHIEF
Courtesy: Nebraska State Historical Society, Lincoln, Nebraska.

LITTLE RAVEN, ARAPAHOE CHIEF
Courtesy: Kansas State Historical Society, Topeka, Kansas.

THOMAS ALDERDICE
Courtesy: James Page, Lincoln, Kansas.
Photographed by: Richard Strublestud

Alderdice, a rugged Kansas frontiersman, was one of the famed Forsythe scouts at Beecher's Island. He was married to Susan (Ziegler) Daly, who was captured by Indians at Spillman Creek.

PEDER CHRISTIANSEN, 1879
Courtesy: A. Virgil Christiansen
Lincoln, Kansas

One of the survivors of the Spillman Creek Massacre, May 30, 1869. A blacksmith from Denmark, he, his brother, Lorentz, and their families arrived in Lincoln, Kansas, in February, 1869.

EDWIN F. TOWNSEND
Courtesy: Kansas State Historical Society Topeka, Kansas.

At the time of the Summit Springs battle, Major Townsend of the U. S. 9th Infantry was commander at Fort Sedgwick, Colorado.

WILLIAM HATFIELD
Courtesy: Overland Trail Museum Sterling, Colorado

In 1871, the first permanent settler arrived at Summit Springs, Sterling, Colorado. He was 32 years old, and was from Derbyshire, England.

SUMMIT SPRINGS MONUMENT

Courtesy: Overland Trail Museum, Sterling, Colorado.

Located in the gently rolling sand hills and wind-swept plains of northeastern Colorado beside a tiny stream called White Butte Creek, Summit Springs is so named because of a fine spring of water on the summit of the hills. It is in an obscure and out of the way place between the Platte River and the Frenchmen Creek where no one would suspect there would be fresh water. It was a favorite camping ground of the renegade plains Indians in the 1860's.

INDIAN SKETCH BOOK CAPTURED AT SUMMIT SPRINGS

Courtesy: Library, State Historical Society of Colorado

At the battle of Summit Springs, in one of the Indian lodges, a notebook of over a hundred pictographs was found. The ledger book, illustrated by a Cheyenne artist, contains sketches of Indian warriors in combat with whites and enemy tribesmen. Included are depictions of the Kidder Annihilation and the Beecher Island Battle.

"OUR LANDS ARE WHERE OUR DEAD LIE BURIED"

IN RECOGNITION

of an unknown fifteen-year old Cheyenne herdboy who was slain in the conflict at Summit Springs, July 11, 1869. He was killed while stampeding the horses into the Indian village, thus enabling many of his people to escape. Luther North, Army Scout, said of the heroic youth: "No braver man ever lived."

Chief Tall Bull, Heavy Furred Wolf, Pile of Bones, Lone Bear, Black Sun, White Rock, Big Gip, Powder Face and forty-five Cheyenne and Sioux men, women and children also died here.

Richard Tall Bull (great grandson of Chief Tall Bull) came to this place on July 11, 1969 and prayed that the Indian nations might live. He pleaded that all men "live in harmony and respect one another."

This monument erected by concerned members of both the red and white races in the Moon of Black Cherries.

AUGUST 1970

INSCRIPTION ON MONUMENT AT SUMMIT SPRINGS

PART III

CHAPTER 10

CHRONOLOGY

The chronology that follows is an outline of the frontier history of the Central Plains; of the whiteman and the Southern Cheyenne Indian encounters. Whenever the Indian is mentioned, it will be this tribe, and more specifically the famed Dog Soldier (Hotamitanui) warriors of this tribe. They were the most feared band on the Plains.

The Dog Soldiers were especially valuable during the Plains Indian wars of the late 1800's. Their reckless bravery and fanatic-like dedication inspired other Indians. They typified the Indian attitude it is bad to live to be old, better to die young fighting bravely in battle. War and hunting were very important to the Plains Indians. The Dog Soldiers did not wear the common war bonnet of eagle feathers, but rather a bonnet of crow feathers without the string of feathers hanging down the warrior's back. One of the customs of this band was the use of the dog rope. It was the sash of a buffalo skin several feet long with a wooden picket pin at the end. When caught in a desperate situation, the warrior drove the pin into the ground. He would have to stay there until he was either killed, or his people drove the enemy away.

The Central Plains, for this text, is that general area along the Platte and Republican Rivers in southwestern Nebraska and southern Wyoming, the South Platte in Colorado, and the Smoky Hills-Saline-Solomon Rivers in Western Kansas.

Geographically, the Platte River divides the Great Plains into two regions, the northern plains and the southern plains.

Its tributaries originate in the snows of the rugged Colorado Rocky Mountains. It rushes out of the mountains a few miles southwest of Denver. Flowing through Denver, it picks up Cherry Creek, and near Greeley, it is joined by the Poudre River. With a wide valley meandering eastward, its waters are in places shallow and a mile wide and in others, a mere thread.

The river valley was the route of the moving Indian tribes, of trappers, of traders, of John Fremont, of Stephen Long, of gold seekers and, finally, of settlers.

The Platte River trail was a path that saw the greatest western migration in American history. The travelers were not driven so much by famine, war, or persecution as by their own free will in search of land, gold, wealth, and adventure. The great trail was called the Oregon Trail, the Platte Road, the California Trail, or the Great Medicine Road. It eventually dictated the course of the railroads and, thereafter, routes of highways.

In 1869, the rich bottom lands and tall grass of the Platte Valley were a sportsman's paradise. Along with the buffalo were herds of antelope, geese, ducks and sandhill cranes. In the rolling sandhills, which border the valley, were many prairie chicken, grouse and sage hen. Author Washington Irving, while visiting the frontier West, described the stream as the most magnificent and most useless of all rivers.

The Republican River was a traditional buffalo hunting ground for the Plains Indians. It was also a favorite camping ground for them in the 1860's and served as a haven of safety for raids against the overland trails and the construction crews of the Union Pacific and Kansas Pacific railroads. Unlike many plains rivers, the Republican has numerous steepbanked and wooded tributaries. Springfed streams meander back into the hill country for several miles, providing the Indians with concealed, sheltered camps. Being in the heart of a major buffalo range, well stocked with other wild game, it was perfect Indian country, while unfavorable for normal military operations.

In the days of the first settlers, the Saline and Solomon Valleys were often visited by marauding bands of Indians who killed or carried away the whiteman and destroyed his property. The Spillman Creek territory, which is now Lincoln County, Kansas, was considered unsafe. The farmers in the 1860's lived in constant alertness of the Indian. While the primary object of their raids was to get food and plunder, the nature of the reckless, young Indian warriors did not always let them stop at merely compelling pioneers to cook for them and to give up their valuables.

Because of the unusual stone fence posts the area would one day be known as "land of the post rock."

The redmen-whitemen encounters begin.

1541– Coronado, the Spanish explorer, came north to the Colorado-Kansas plains searching for the seven cities of gold, Cibola. No gold was found and the high plains were forgotten for almost two centuries. However, the conquistadors brought with them an animal that would eventually change the way of life of the Cheyenne Indians, the horse. Also, in the valleys of the Platte, Republican, and Arkansas Rivers, they found in great herds, the King of prairie and plain, the humpbacked American buffalo.

There is a cave in a bluff south of Lincoln Center, Kansas, that settlers would one day discover. The Spaniards engraved a dart, a fish, a beaver, and a sage hen on the cave wall.

1695- Governor Don Diego de Vargas, Spanish New Mexico, wrote a letter that complicates the first date of the Cheyenne Indian on the Central Plains. He wrote to Spain that a band of Apaches from the East called "Chiyenes" visited his city.

1720– The Spanish sent a reconnaissance party up to the South Platte River to find the location of the French who they had learned had been in contact with the Pawnee Indians, the hated enemies of the Cheyenne. Frenchmen had been on the

Platte with the Pawnee at the turn of the eighteenth century, but these rough, devil-may-care (coureur de bois) French trappers and traders left few records. It was not until the educated Frenchman, Bourgmont, had written considerable material about his experiences with the Pawnee Indians that the Spanish became alarmed. The expedition headed by Villusur traveled up from New Mexico looking for the French. Near the forks of the Platte, the hostile Pawnee armed with French weapons, ambushed Villusur's party killing thirty-two of the forty-two soldiers, including Villusur. Explorer, scout, and Indian fighter, Naranjo, who is reported to have named the South Platte River, Rio De Jesus Maria, was also killed. The French were aroused that a Spanish military expedition had found its way almost to the Missouri. This produced considerable talk in Paris and plans were made to destroy any further Spanish forces to the Platte.

1739– The Mallet brothers, French explorers, with a party of Canadian traders came from eastern Nebraska along the Missouri River to obtain information about the route to New Mexico. They penetrated eastern Colorado, went up the South Platte River, and then turned southward. Though the Spanish discovered it, these Frenchmen are generally credited with having given the modern day name Platte, meaning dull and shallow, to the river.

1780– Four years after the Declaration of Independence by the United States, the great smallpox epidemic struck the Plains Indians. With new tribes pushing into the plains, it was the catalyst in the dawning of the modern times on the plains. The old Plains Indian tribes, reduced in number by the disease and with few firearms, were driven southward by newcomers. The Cheyenne were one of the last of these plains tribes to reach the high, central plains. In the middle of the eighteenth century, the Cheyenne had moved westward to the Missouri and built villages.

They were followed by the Sioux armed with guns and eventually, to avoid the Sioux annoyance, took to roaming. They left their villages and cultivated fields. They moved near the Black Hills where they met the Arapahoe and obtained horses. Soon after the epidemic, the Southern Cheyenne and the Arapahoe were found in the area between the Platte and Arkansas Rivers between Central Kansas and the Rocky Mountains. They roamed and wandered nomadically over the barren hills hunting buffalo and other game. They made their villages along streams and rivers and made war upon enemy tribes such as the Ute to the west in the Rocky Mountains and the Pawnee to the east.

1790 – The frontier of the gun from the French in the east, and the horse frontier moving up from the Spanish in the south, meshed on the Great Plains. This fusion provided the Cheyenne and other Plains Indians with the means to make a formidable barrier to the whiteman's expansion into the western frontier. Indians of the Central Plains and the Rocky Mountains, numbering about a quarter of a million people, were a definite obstacle to white settlement. The United States, numbering seventeen states at this time, had a population of less than four million. The strongest and most war-like Indian nations were the Sioux, Blackfoot, Crow, Cheyenne, Arapahoe, Nez Perces, Ute, Comanche, Apache, and Kiowa. Mounted on swift horses, well armed for plains warfare, and living off the buffalo that roamed the open range these tribes would maintain stubborn resistance to penetration of their hunting grounds.

1806 – Three years after the Louisiana Purchase, twenty-seven year old Zebulon Pike came to Colorado to explore. The young army officer was the first Englishman to southern Colorado to describe Pikes Peak. At the time that Pike was heading west on his expedition, the famed Lewis and Clark Expedition was on its way homeward. Lewis and Clark traversed the northern regions of the Louisiana Purchase to the Pacific Coast. They had encountered Cheyenne Indians in the Black Hills and had presented them with the American flag and trinkets. Pike was temporarily delayed by the Spaniards, who escorted him to Santa Fe where he found James Purcell. Purcell, a Frenchman, told him he had been trading with Cheyenne Indians in the South Platte and South Park area for several years.

1820 – Eight years after the new nation's second war with England, Major Stephen Long was sent to northeastern Colorado to locate the source of the Platte River. Upon first view of the Rockies from the South Platte Valley, Long and his party sighted Long's Peak. He labeled the high plains east of the Rocky Mountains the Great American Desert, a land that would never sustain an agricultural society, only buffalo and the Indian. Long, a railroad engineer, later wrote one of the first textbooks on railroading in the United States. Vision of agricultural irrigation and technology escaped him.

1833 – Bents Fort, a trading post, was built on the Santa Fe Trail on the banks of the Arkansas River. Two years later, the first trading post on the South Platte Valley, Fort Vasquez, was established by mountain men Vasquez and St. Vrain. These Indian trading posts were the only permanent buildings or settlements in Colorado. By the mid-1800's, the best days of the beaver trade were gone. The buffalo trade could not support these small trading posts and most posts along the Platte Valley were deserted.

1842 – The Pathfinder, handsome, twenty-nine year old John Fremont, was sponsored with a federal grant to map the major trails over the Rocky Mountains to the Pacific Coast. He was fortunate in employing the renowned Kit Carson and Broken Hand Fitzpatrick as his guides. The long Oregon Trail, leading up the Platte River and across the South Pass through Cheyenne Indian country on the way to the rich agricultural land of Oregon, required this survey for better maps, trails and sites for military posts to protect travelers. Also, it took a month for mail via Panama, to reach California from New York and a practical overland route was required.

Up to the mid-1800's, traffic into the Central Plains, the land of the Cheyenne Indians, was largely trappers, traders, and explorers. Then the migrants to Oregon in their covered wagons became a familiar sight. Initially the migration was insignificant, one thousand in 1843, three times that in 1845, then approximately forty thousand in the California Gold Rush of 1849. The Indians were becoming increasingly alarmed. The whitemen not only brought diseases but they destroyed or frightened away the game. After the Mexican War in 1848, more and more restless "soldiers of fortune" arrived in the West.

1851 – The Fitzpatrick Treaty, also called the Treaty of 1851 or Treaty of Ft. Laramie, to promote peace between the Plains Indians and the white people, was signed. The total number of Cheyenne, Arapahoe, Sioux, Crow and other tribes present for the signing at Fort Laramie was approximately ten thousand. The land between the Platte and the Arkansas east of the Rockies was assigned to the Cheyenne and Arapahoe. Shortly after the treaty, the Cheyenne (Tsistsistas) nation split into two divisions; the Southern division and the Northern division. In the treaty the Indians did not surrender the privilege of hunting, fishing, or passing over any of the high plains. They were free to hunt and war among themselves, but their days of freedom were numbered. Within ten years the whiteman would begin to claim their lands.

The United States was now a nation of over 23 million people and included thirty-seven states. Arizona, Colorado, Idaho, Kansas, Montana, Nebraska, Nevada, North and South Dakota, Oklahoma, West Virginia, Wyoming as well as Alaska and Hawaii were not yet states.

1854 – The all out war to suppress the Plains Indians began over a broken-down, scraggly stray cow belonging to an immigrant Morman, and ended in the annihilation of Lieutenant Grattan and his men. Young Grattan, twenty-four years old, Irish and a U. S. Army officer, was boastful, hot headed and rough. Prior to what is known as the Grattan Massacre, he stated that with a dozen soldiers he could whip the entire Cheyenne nation. Grattan and twenty-eight of his men were killed and mutilated when they rode into a Sioux Indian camp demanding retribution for the cow. Grattan's body was filled with twenty-four arrows. In retaliation a year later, General Harney with 600 soldiers attacked Little Thunder's Sioux village at Ash Hollow, killing 86 and capturing seventy Indian women and children.

A brave, young Cheyenne Dog Soldier, named Tall Bull, was emerging as a leader. His mother was a Sioux and he had two Indian names, Tatonkahaska and Hotuaehkaashtait. He played a significant role as a scout for his tribe when they tried to recover their sacred medicine arrows from their hated rivals, the Pawnee.

1856 – The tall, handsome Cheyenne, a well-mounted and fearless tribe, were constantly fighting with neighboring Indian tribes, but traditionally were friendly to the whiteman. Only a few Cheyenne were present at the Grattan battle and they did not have their first real encounter with the whiteman until 1856. One day in April, near the Platte Bridge, Casper, Wyoming, they fought with the U. S. Army over four horses reportedly stolen. One Indian and an old trapper were the casualties of the conflict. In June they made a revengeful attack on an immigrant wagon train. Two months later real trouble began. After an attack by Captain Stewart, the Cheyenne started a complete, savage raid of the Platte River trail, killing and plundering. Almon Babbitt, secretary of Utah Territory, was one of the many whitemen killed. After their attacks the Cheyenne left the Platte for the Republican River.

1857 – Colonel (Bull of the Woods) Sumner, with about four hundred cavalry and infantry, supported by four mountain howitzers, routed a large party of Cheyenne warriors near the Solomon River. It was one of few occasions when a large body of troops charged Indians with flashing sabres. Nine Indian warriors were killed and many wounded in the brief skirmish and chase. The soldiers lost two men. Though casualties were small, the Indians lost most of their equipment, food, and lodges, as well as a year's annuity goods.

1858 – All Indians of the Central Plains except the Kiowa were quiet. The Cheyenne were anxious for a treaty after their unhappy encounter the previous fall with Colonel Sumner. Most believed it was useless to fight against so many whitemen. Because the whitemen would soon occupy much of the plains and because the buffalo were diminishing, the older chiefs wished for peace. They hoped the United States would give them a home, free from whiteman's encroachment, where they could be provided for until they were taught to be farmers.

However, Russell Green, at the convergence of the South Platte River and Cherry Creek, discovered gold and white immigrants swarmed up the Platte, Arkansas, and Republican Rivers. The gold rush to the Colorado Rocky Mountains ignited a stampede equivalent to the California Gold Rush of 1849. Only this time the whites did not pass on through the Colorado mountains and plains. Instead they built settlements and settled down to stay. The Leavenworth and Pikes Peak Express Company established stage lines along the Republican River, the very heart of the Cheyenne hunting ground.

1859 – By Spring, the Platte River travel was very heavy, approximately one hundred-fifty thousand people. Denver City, at the base of the Rockies, was thriving. The name of Colorado had not yet officially emerged and it was not a territory or state. An uneasy calm existed on the plains during the winter of 1859-60. Indian agent William Bent pressed hard for a continuation of negotiations for a treaty.

1860 – The Southern Arkansas River Indians, including Black Kettle, Chief of the Southern Cheyenne, met with Commissioner Greenwood, Bureau of Indian Affairs, and were essentially agreeable to his proposals. In the new treaty he would prepare, they would consent to a reservation greatly reduced from the Fort Laramie Treaty.

1861 – Indian agent Albert Boone, Daniel Boone's grandson, was instrumental in getting several chiefs of the Southern Cheyenne and Arapahoe Indians to Fort Wise in February. Here on the Arkansas River, United States' officials, the peace leaders of the Cheyenne, and Little Raven of the Arapahoe, signed the new treaty. However, many of the Cheyenne, including the Platte River band and the Dog Soldiers, refused to sign stating that they would never settle on a reservation. It was the understanding of the chiefs that they would retain their land rights and freedom of movement to hunt buffalo, but that they would live within a triangular section of territory bounded by Sand Creek and the Arkansas River. Freedom of movement was an especially vital matter because the reservation assigned to the two tribes had almost no wild game on it. For their land the Indians would receive $450,000 over a fifteen year period. President Lincoln did not proclaim the treaty effective until December 15th. Meanwhile, the Civil War broke out.

In October, the completion of the telegraph line between St. Joseph and the Pacific Coast brought an end to the short-lived, experimental pony express.

1862 – News reached the people of Colorado that there was a massive Sioux uprising in Minnesota killing many whites. The inter-tribal Indian warfare, the Cheyenne fighting the Ute or Pawnee, and the Arapahoe, friends of the Cheyenne, the Kiowa, constantly going on in Colorado had always been troublesome. War parties of each tribe made frequent trips into white settlements and many times stole horses as well as food. The settlers were becoming increasingly uneasy and alarmed. Colonel Leavenworth and a company of the Second Colorado Volunteers chased a band of Cheyenne who had been raiding along the South Platte River to their Republican River hideout and increased tensions. Governor Evans of Colorado Territory was sure that the Central Plains Indians were intending to start an Indian war in Colorado.

1863 – Prior to the mid-1800's, the barrier of the Rocky Mountains had deflected the westward overland routes around Colorado along the Oregon Trail in the north, and the Santa Fe Trail in the south. After the '58 Gold Rush, transportation and mail service went to Colorado mostly by the Overland Stage Coach along the South Platte River. The telegraph line was completed from Julesburg to Denver.

1864 – At Fremont's Orchard along the South Platte, a fight took place in April, between a small party of Cheyenne and the Colorado Volunteers led by Lieutenant Dunn. The Volunteers were out looking for stolen horses. In May, Major Downing and the First Colorado Cavalry, at Cedar Canyon north of the South Platte, killed several Indians including women and children. They destroyed their village and captured hundreds of horses. They took no prisoners. Lieutenant Eayre was sent from Camp Weld into Kansas to hunt Indians in June. His troops captured Crow Chief's camp and burned all the lodges. They were camped on the head of the Republican where they had just finished their winter buffalo hunting.

Shortly thereafter, a band of renegade Indians killed the Hungate family near Denver. Hungate, his wife, and two children were scalped and mutilated. The women were raped. Their bloody bodies were brought to Denver and placed in public view causing great hositility toward the Cheyenne. All indications were that the Arapahoe, and not the Cheyenne, were the culprits.

In July, the Indians captured horses near Camp Sanborne (Ft. Morgan) as well as the Bijou Ranch on the South Platte. They also killed whitemen and took stock from Junction Ranch. The Indians killed several men, and carried off a woman and a boy near Plum Creek in August. That same month a large Cheyenne village on the Solomon River was urged by William Bent to make peace with the whites and meet with Governor Evans as he had been requesting. They discussed it, decided to talk to Evans, and contacted their Indian agent, Wynkoop.

Captain N. J. O'Brien with Company "F" of the Seventh Iowa Cavalry, was sent to guard the South Platte Road in the neighborhood of Julesburg. Shortly thereafter in September, he was ordered by General Mitchell to build Fort Sedgwick and to stay for the coming winter. He purchased from Samuel Bancroft an adobe house and corral a short distance from the small frontier town of Julesburg. Using sod, the soldiers built a stockade around the house, their barracks, and stables.

In October, Captain Nichols of the Colorado Third, stationed at Valley Station (Sterling), took forty men and surprised two lodges of Cheyenne Indians on White Butte Creek (Wohkpoominoinos) at Summit Springs. They killed all Indians including Big Wolf, the chief, five warriors, three women, and one teenage boy.

By this time Wynkoop had taken the Indians desiring to make peace to Denver, and thereafter, to Fort Lyon. He had promised them that if they moved to Sand Creek near Fort Lyon, negotiations could commence. In November, however, Wynkoop was relieved of his duties at Fort Lyon and replaced by Major Scott J. Anthony, an officer of Chivington's Colorado Volunteers. Black Kettle, main chief and leader of the peace seeking Cheyenne, had been thinking of moving far south of the Arkansas so that they would feel safe from the soldiers. But Major Anthony said he would continue Wynkoop's policy and they would be safe at Sand Creek for the winter. The Cheyenne stayed.

Six hundred men of Colonel Chivington's Colorado regiments, including most of the Third, under sanction of Governor John Evans, reached Fort Lyon from Denver. They surrounded the fort and forbid anyone to leave. Bolstered by Anthony's soldiers, Chivington, a sometime preacher, marched on to Big Sandy (Sand Creek). Beckworth and the eldest son of William Bent were forced to be guides.

At daybreak, November 29, Chivington attacked the friendly Cheyenne village. Under the Indians' white flag of truce, soldiers shot, scalped and mutilated men, women, and children, who begged for mercy.

As news of the Sand Creek Massacre spread across the plains, the Cheyenne sent out runners with messages calling for a war of revenge against the murdering whitemen. The Dog Soldiers, under Tall Bull, who refused to go to the Sand Creek camp were joined by their great war warrior, Roman Nose and the Arapahoe, the Northern Cheyenne, and the Sioux under Spotted Tail and Pawnee Killer. While the Cheyenne mourned their dead, the war leaders of the tribes smoked war pipes and planned their strategy. They outlined a policy of continuous harrassment. Black Kettle, who miraculously survived the massacre, was rejected. He moved his survivors south into Comanche territory.

In this few hours of madness, Chivington destroyed the power of every Cheyenne chief who had held out for peace with the whitemen. He united all Indians on the Central Plains as well as the Comanche, Apache, Kiowa and the Ute who traditionally hated the Plains Indians more than they did the newly arrived whites.

For Colorado the winter of 1864 was the start of an unrelenting reign of terror. A long and bitter war had started; not the usual depredations by isolated renegade bands of Indians. The war would include a united force of all Central Plains

Indians who had by now convinced themselves that the Great Spirit had the whitemen fighting each other so that they could take their land back. They would raid nearly every stage station, ranch and settlement between the forks of the Platte and Denver, killing, burning and devastating every mile along the way. They would tear down the telegraph lines, paralyze passenger and food supply lines, and earn for Colorado and western Kansas the reputation as the most dangerous area in the United States. Immigrants, waiting at the Missouri River, would refuse to travel overland. Mail from the east would again be routed by way of Panama to California and Oregon. Denver would be virtually isolated from the rest of the country.

Four of the first settlers in Lincoln County, Kansas, fought and killed several Indians near the cave on Bull-Foot Creek. The settlers, John Moffit, Thomas Moffit, John Housten and James Tyler, were all eventually killed.

1865 – In early January, twelve hundred Cheyenne with bands of Arapahoe and Sioux made an attack on Julesburg and Fort Sedgwick, garrisoned by the Seventh Cavalry. The Indians lured the soldiers away from the fort. They annihilated those soldiers that could not return to the fort after their decoy party led them into the main body of Indian warriors hiding in the sand hills. The soldiers lost sixteen men. Fifty Indians were killed. Later, a second attack was made and Julesburg was burned. After their return from the attack on Julesburg, the Indians broke camp on Cherry Creek of the Republican and some moved north to Summit Springs. The chiefs of the three tribes decided to make another great raid along the South Platte and then join the Northern Cheyenne and Sioux on the Powder River. A youthful Sitting Bull was assisting Sioux chiefs Spotted Tail and Pawnee Killer at this time.

They raided and plundered up and down the Platte Valley route, halting all communications and travel. They set fire to the prairies, and for over fifty miles along the Platte it looked very much like a war zone.* In Denver there was a food shortage. After this destruction, they crossed the river and, in February, went into camp near Julesburg prior to moving north.

When they reached the Powder River country, the Southern Cheyenne were welcomed by their kinsmen, the Northern Cheyenne under Dull Knife, as well as by the Sioux, under Red Cloud. This alliance made several attacks on whites. During one of these encounters, Roman Nose's brother was killed and he became angry for revenge.

Lee surrendered to Grant in April and the Civil War was over. Many from the U. S. Army would soon become Indian fighters.

In October, Black Kettle of the Southern Cheyenne and Little Raven of the Arapahoe met the United States commissioners, including Kit Carson and William Bent, at the mouth of the Little Arkansas. Along with other chiefs desiring peace, they signed a new treaty agreeing to perpetual peace. In this treaty, Black Kettle and the Southern Cheyenne abandoned claims to their tribal land in the rich buffalo country between the Platte and Arkansas Rivers in the Colorado Territory. No other divisions or bands of the Cheyenne were represented. Only 80 of about 300 lodges of Southern Cheyenne were present. From its inception, there was little chance that this treaty would end any wars on the Central Plains.

* Included in the South Platte raids were attacks on Beaver Creek Station, Harlow's Ranch, Valley Station, Godfrey's Ranch, the American Ranch, the Wisconsin Ranch, Washington Ranch, Lillian Springs Ranch, Moore's Ranch, Gittrell's Ranch, Buffalo Springs Ranch, Springs Hill Station, and Buler's Ranch. Of these, only Godfrey repelled the onslaught, earning the name Fort Wicked.

1866 – As the Sioux under Red Cloud were preparing to fight for the Powder River country, a considerable number of Southern Cheyenne decided to go south for the summer. They wanted to hunt buffalo along their beloved Central Plains, and to see their old friends and relatives who had gone with

Black Kettle below the Arkansas. Among them were Tall Bull, White Horse, and other Dog Soldier chiefs. The great war leader, Roman Nose, also went along as did the two half-breed Bent brothers. They went into Kansas to hunt against the decrees of the Arkansas Treaty. Fresh from the freedom and independence of the Powder River country, the Dog Soldier chiefs scoffed at the Treaty. None of them had signed it, none accepted it, and they had no use for chiefs who signed away tribal rights to their old hunting grounds.

Indian agent Wynkoop learned that the Dog Soldiers were again hunting on the Central Plains. He went to them and tried to persuade them to sign the treaty and join Black Kettle. They refused. Wynkoop warned them that soldiers would probably attack them if they stayed in Kansas, but they replied that they would never leave their country again. They would live or die here. The Dog Soldiers had been hearing encouraging rumors of Red Cloud's successes against the soldiers in the Powder River country. The Sioux and Northern Cheyenne were fighting to hold their country. They would do the same. Faced with a long winter, the Southern Cheyenne and Arapahoe came together. They decided to make a permanent camp on the Republican and make plans to stop travel along the western Kansas roads next spring.

In December, Captain Fetterton was ambushed and annihilated by Red Cloud's Sioux and some Cheyenne outside Fort Phil Kearney, Wyoming. Seventy-nine of his men and two civilians were killed. It was the opinion of Dr. Horton, the post surgeon who examined the bodies after the bloody encounter, that the Sioux were still largely armed with the bow and arrow since not more than six soldiers were killed by bullets. The Fetterman battle made a deep impression on the United States government. It was the worst defeat the Army had yet suffered in Indian warfare, and the second in American history from which came no survivors. Fetterman thought as little of Indian warriors as Grattan, and had similarly boasted that with 80 men he could ride through the whole Sioux nation.

It would take two years of resistance, but Red Cloud and the Sioux would win their war. Fort Smith and Fort Phil Kearney would be abandoned and the Powder River road would be officially closed to travel by whitemen. Red Cloud was a model for all Indians resentful of the U. S. Army or the reservation.

Elsewhere in the world, the South German states joined Otto Von Bismarck's Prussia and the North German states to form the North German Confederation. Prussia and Austria turned on each other, ending in Austria's defeat and they left the German Confederation. Amongst this turmoil, a young Prussian couple married. A pretty eighteen year old girl named Maria became the wife of George Weichel, twenty-eight years old and an upcoming brewer.

1867 - Spring, the U. S. government sent word to the Indian agents to assemble their tribes for council. Wynkoop induced the Cheyenne Dog Soldier leaders to come to Fort Larned and hear what General Winfield Scott Hancock had to say. Tall Bull, White Horse, Bull Bear, Whirlwind, and other chiefs grudgingly brought about five hundred lodges down to Pawnee Creek. After making camp near Fort Larned, the Indian warriors rode on into the fort. Here Tall Bull made his famous speech to Hancock. The tall, commanding chief lit a pipe, exhaled smoke, and passed it around. He stood, folded his red and black blanket to free his right arm, and offering his hand to Hancock, said:

> "You sent for us. We came here. We never did the whiteman any harm. We don't intend to. Our agent Colonel Wynkoop, told us to meet you here. Whenever you want to go to the Smoky Hill you can go; you can go on any road. When we come on the road, your young men must not shoot us. We are willing to be friends with the whiteman. The buffalo are diminishing fast. The antelope, that were plenty a few years ago, they are now thin. When they shall all die we shall be hungry; we shall

want something to eat, and we will be compelled to come into the fort. Your young men must not fire at us; whenever they see us they fire, and we fire on them. You say you are going to our village tomorrow. If you go, I shall have no more to say to you there than here. I have said all I want to say."

Hancock had arrogantly told the Indians he was going to take his troops to their village the next day. They distrusted him and were afraid of another Sand Creek. The news that the soldiers were coming stirred the Indian camp into immediate action. There was no time to dismantle the lodges or pack. They put the women and children on horses and sent them racing northward. Then all the warriors armed themselves with bows, lances, guns, knives, and clubs, and went out to delay Hancock's movement. The chiefs named Roman Nose, their war leader, to talk to Hancock. Bull Bear rode beside him to make sure that in his anger he did nothing foolish since he had previously stated that he would kill the arrogant Hancock. After Roman Nose and Hancock talked, the Indians retreated. Although the chiefs and warriors obediently rode away in the direction their women and children had taken, they did not bring them back as Hancock had demanded. Nor did they return. Hancock waited, his anger rising, for two days. He then marched into the Indian camp and found it deserted. The Indians had fled.

His soldiers burned and destroyed the village. Hancock then sent Custer out to try to find the Indians who had fled. Failing to locate any Indians, Custer left the Republican Valley and headed north. He crossed the Platte near Fort Sedgwick, where he learned that while he had been on the Republican, Lieutenant Kidder with ten men and an Indian guide had been sent with new orders. Custer never received these orders, nor saw any signs of Kidder. Custer then set out from the Platte, reaching Beaver Creek on the Republican. In a little hollow, his column found Lieutenant Kidder and all his men lying dead among the tall grasses. They had been ambushed and annihilated by the Sioux and Cheyenne.

The rage of the Dog Soldiers and their Sioux allies at the burning of their village was felt across the plains. All out war returned to the Central Plains. The Indians again raided settlements, tore down telegraph lines, attacked railroaders, stage stations, and brought travel to a halt along the Kansas roads. General Custer's summer campaign on the Republican River was futile and the Indians continued to raid unchecked on the Central Plains of Colorado, Kansas and Nebraska. Sherman was persuaded by higher government authorities to bring peace back to the plains. In the summer he formed the commission of Taylor, Henderson, Tappan, Sanborn, Harney, and Terry to make another treaty with the Plains Indians. The blundering Hancock was recalled from the plains, and his soldiers were scattered among forts along the trails. He was replaced by General Sheridan.

The new peace plan included not only the Southern Cheyenne and Arapahoe but the Kiowa, Comanche, and Apache. All five tribes would be established on one great reservation south of the Arkansas River, and the government would provide them with cattle herds and teach them how to grow crops. Medicine Lodge Creek was chosen as the site of a peace council. The meetings were held early in October. George Bent, now employed as an interpreter by Wynkoop, was one of the emissaries. He had no difficulty in persuading Black Kettle of the Cheyenne, Little Raven of the Arapahoe, and Ten Bears of the Comanche to travel to Medicine Lodge Creek, but he found the Dog Soldiers reluctant to listen. After much delay, they finally did come to the talks. Several thousand Indians from the Apache, Kiowa, Comanche, Cheyenne, and Arapahoe tribes assembled in southern Kansas for the council. H. M Stanley, a correspondent with the New York Herald, later to become famous as an African explorer, was a reporter for the talks.

On October 28, the Cheyenne leaders consented to the

Medicine Lodge Treaty and signed it, but with noticeable hesitation and dismay. The hostile Dog Soldiers had been convinced that their tribe's best future lay in the proposed reservation below the Arkansas. Most of the Cheyenne would move south as they had promised. There were others, however, who would not go. Over a hundred were already heading north with a warrior who would not surrender. He was not a chief and had not signed the treaty. Roman Nose, the war leader, would fight to the death for his beloved Plains.

In the fall of 1867, a rare state of peace existed on the Central Plains, but only briefly.

1868 - At the first of the year most of the Southern Cheyenne were camped below the Arkansas near Fort Larned. From their fall hunts they had enough meat to survive the cold winter but by springtime a food shortage was imminent. The U. S. government had not provided enough money to buy all the food, clothing, guns and ammunition as promised. Considerable whiskey was available in trade for their furs. Drunkeness was commonplace and did the uneasy situation no good. The young warriors grew increasingly restless, grumbling about their miserable, desolate reservations and cursed the broken promises of the whiteman. In small bands they began drifting northward toward their old hunting grounds.

One day in the summer, near present day Denmark, Lincoln County, Kansas, three women by the names of Bacon, Foster and Shaw were taken captive by the Indians. After a week of abuse and raping, they were released more dead than alive. They would serve as a warning for the Kansas immigrants of 1869.

Tall Bull and White Horse gave in to demands of their proud young Dog Soldiers and also crossed the Arkansas to join Roman Nose. Along the way some of the unruly young men raided isolated settlements. By late August most of these Cheyenne were gathered along the Arickaree Fork of the Republican River. Tall Bull, White Horse, and Roman Nose were there with about three hundred warriors and their families. A few Arapahoes and Pawnee Killer's Sioux were also camped nearby.

In September, a hunting party of Sioux saw about fifty white-men moving up the Arickaree about twenty miles below the Indian camps. The men were dressed in rough frontier clothing. They were the special company organized by Sheridan to search out Indian camps. Under the command of Major George Forsyth, they were known as Forsyth's Scouts. Rugged Thomas Alderdice, from the Kansas frontier, was one of the more experienced members. As soon as the Sioux alerted their people, they sent runners to the Cheyenne camp to ask them to join in an attack on the whites who had invaded their hunting grounds. Tall Bull and White Horse urged their warriors to make ready for war and put on their war paint. The famous battle that followed lasted nine days, and was named for Lieutenant Frederick Beecher who was killed during the battle. The heroic scouts were sieged by eight hundred Cheyenne, Sioux and Arapahoe rushing down from the sand hills. The scouts gallantly warded off attack after attack, and were finally rescued by the U. S. Cavalry. Though casualties were relatively small, the Dog Soldiers' inspirational leader, Roman Nose, was killed, and their morale was crushed.

For the young Cheyenne warriors, the death of Roman Nose was like a great light going out in the sky. They had believed that with him they would fight for their land successfully as Red Cloud's Sioux and the Northern Cheyenne were doing. After they had rested from the siege, many Cheyenne started moving south. With soldiers hunting everywhere, their only hope of survival lay with their tribe below the Arkansas. Black Kettle was a beaten old man, but he was still alive, and he was still the main chief of the Southern Cheyenne. By fall, most of his peaceful Indians were camped on the Washita River not far from Ft. Cobb, Oklahoma. The village contained about seventy-five lodges.

Bearded Civil War hero, Ulysses S. Grant was elected President of the United States.

Suddenly, one cold, foggy November morning, George Custer's troops attacked Black Kettle's village, killing over a hundred Indian men, women and children. Black Kettle did not escape this time. The village was attacked in retaliation for what renegade Indians were doing up north. When news of the Washita massacre and Black Kettle's death reached Tall Bull, depredations on the white settlements increased and took on a new ruthlessness.

MAPS

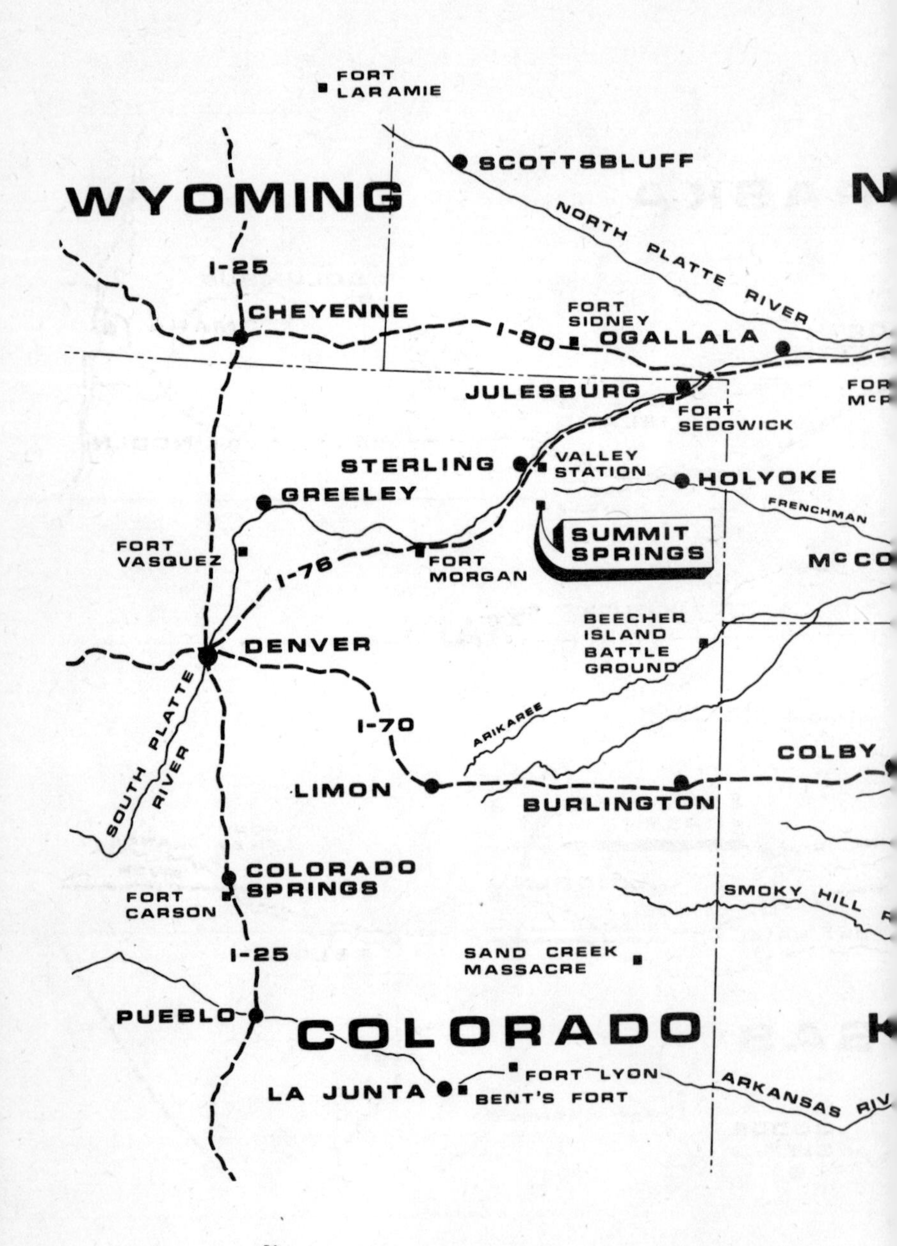
FORT LARAMIE
SCOTTSBLUFF
WYOMING
NORTH PLATTE RIVER
I-25
CHEYENNE
FORT SIDNEY
I-80
OGALLALA
JULESBURG
FORT SEDGWICK
STERLING
VALLEY STATION
HOLYOKE
FRENCHMAN
GREELEY
SUMMIT SPRINGS
FORT VASQUEZ
FORT MORGAN
I-76
BEECHER ISLAND BATTLE GROUND
DENVER
SOUTH PLATTE RIVER
I-70
ARIKAREE
COLBY
LIMON
BURLINGTON
COLORADO SPRINGS
FORT CARSON
SMOKY HILL
I-25
SAND CREEK MASSACRE
PUEBLO
COLORADO
FORT LYON
ARKANSAS
LA JUNTA
BENT'S FORT
CENTRAL

N

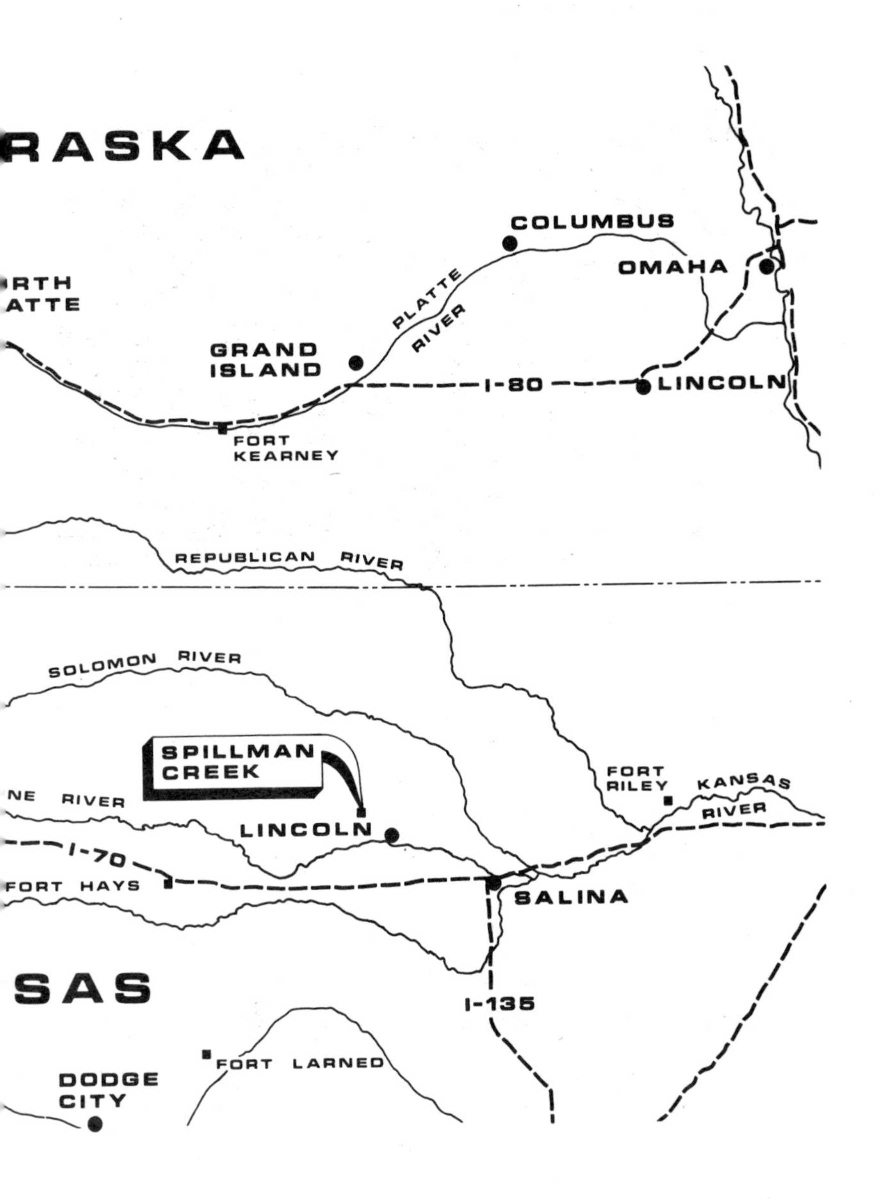
RASKA
COLUMBUS
OMAHA
RTH
ATTE
PLATTE
RIVER
GRAND
ISLAND
I-80
LINCOLN
FORT
KEARNEY
REPUBLICAN RIVER
SOLOMON RIVER
SPILLMAN
CREEK
FORT
RILEY
KANSAS
RIVER
NE RIVER
LINCOLN
I-70
FORT HAYS
SALINA
SAS
I-135
FORT LARNED
DODGE
CITY

PLAINS MAP

1869 EXPEDITIONS

CENTRAL PLAINS

From an official map of the National Archives

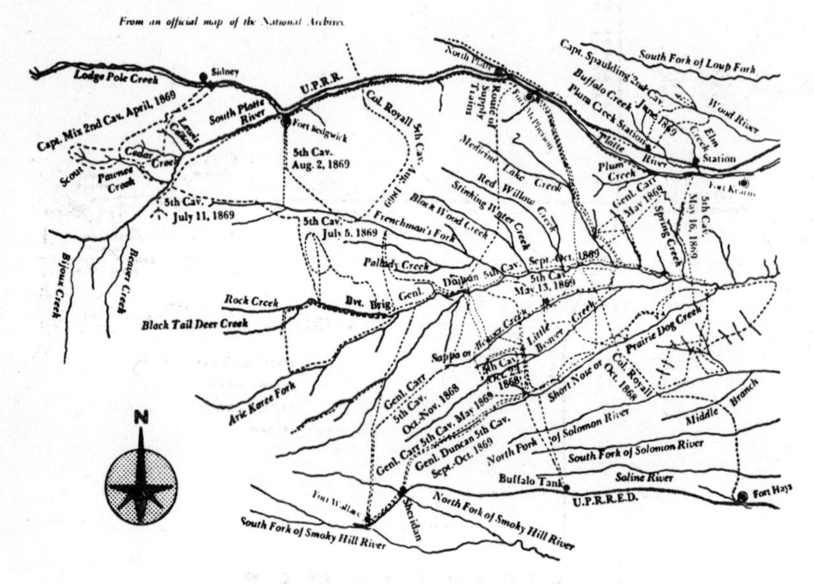

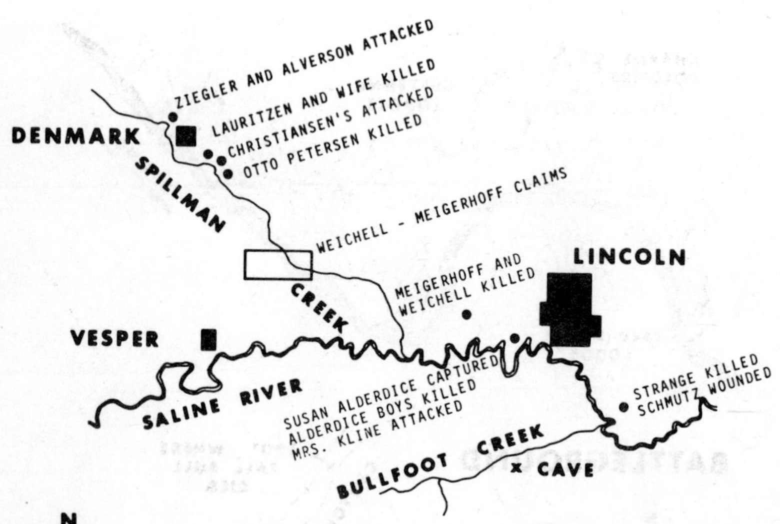

MAP OF MASSACRE

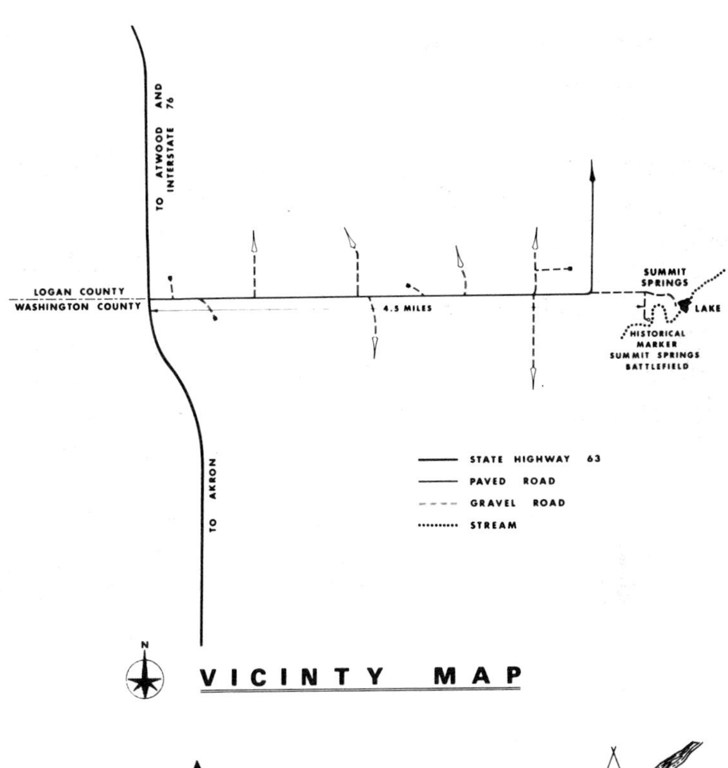

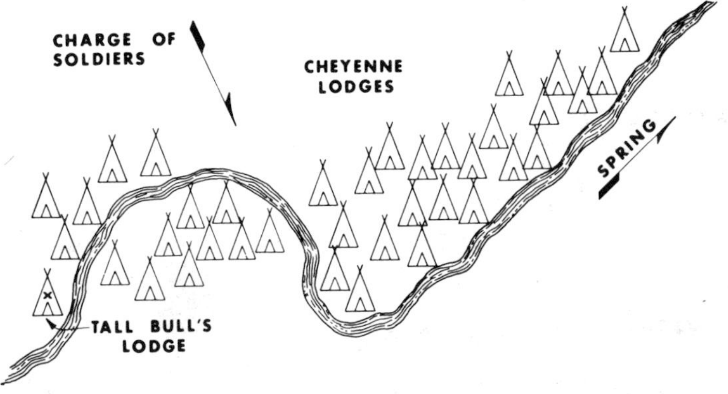

BATTLEGROUND

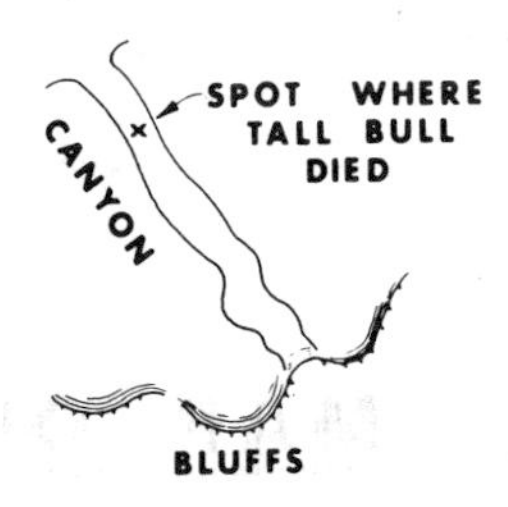

BIBLIOGRAPHY

Allen, Catherine Ward, *Chariot of the Sun,* Maverick Publications, Denver, Colorado, 1976 (Annotated by Harry E. Chrisman).

Athearn, Robert G., "Colorado and the Indian War of 1868", *The Colorado Magazine,* Vol. XXXIII, No. 1, 1956.

Barr, Elizabeth N., *Souvenir History of Lincoln County, Kansas,* Lincoln County Publication, Kansas, 1908.

Bernhardt, C., *Indian Raids, In Lincoln County Kansas,* The Lincoln Sentinel Print, Lincoln, Kansas, 1910.

Berthrong, Donald J., *The Southern Cheyennes,* University of Oklahoma Press, Norman, Oklahoma, 1963.

Brady, Cyrus T., *Indian Fights and Fighters,* McClure-Phillips & Company, 1904, (Reprinted by Bison Books, University of Nebraska Press, Lincoln, 1971).

Bragg, William F., Jr., "Pre-Centennial Campbell County", Speech Delivered at George Amos Library, Casper, Wyo., April, 1976.

Brandes, T. Donald, *Military Posts of Colorado,* The Old Army Press, Ft. Collins, Colorado, 1973.

Brown, Dee, *Bury My Heart at Wounded Knee,* Holt, Rinehart & Winston, New York, New York, 1970.

Carr, Major General E. A., "Famous General Tells of Buffalo Bill's War Service", *The Denver Post,* August, 1908.

Carter, Harvey Lewis, *Dear Old Kit,* University of Oklahoma Press, Norman, 1968.

Cody, William F., *The Life of Honorable William F. Cody,* (An Autobiography), Frank E. Bliss, Hartford, Connecticut, 1879.

Collins, Dabney Otis, *Land of Tall Skies,* Century One Press, Colorado Springs, Colorado, 1977.

Conklin, Emma Burke, *History of Logan County Colorado,* Welch-Haffner Printing Company, Denver, Colorado, 1928.

Craig, Reginald S., "Tall Bull's Last Fight", *Denver Westerners Roundup,* April, 1968.

Custer, General George, *My Life on the Plains,* Sheldon & Company, New York, New York, 1874, University of Oklahoma Press, Norman, 1962.

Dallas, Sandra, *Yesterday's Denver,* E. A. Seeman Publishing Inc., Miami, Florida, 1974.

Danker, Donald F., "The Journal of an Indian Fighter (Frank North)", *Nebraska History,* Vol. 39, No. 2, 1958.

DeVoto, Bernard, *Across the Wide Missouri,* Houghton Mifflin Company, Boston, Massachusetts, 1947.

Dickinson, Alice, *Taken by the Indians,* Franklin Watts, New York, New York, 1976.

Dodge, Colonel Richard I., *Our Wild Indians,* Archer House, Inc., New York, New York, 1883.

Dunn, Ruth, *Indian Vengeance at Julesburg,* Private Publication, 1972.

Ewers, John C., *Artists of the Old West,* Doubleday & Co., Garden City, New York, 1965.

Farrell, Cliff, *The Mighty Land,* Doubleday & Company, Inc., Garden City, New York, 1975.

Filipiak, Jack D., "The Battle of Summit Springs", *The Colorado Magazine,* Vol. XLI, No. 4, 1964.

Fisher, John R., 'The Royall and Duncan Pursuits: Aftermath of the Battle of Summit Springs", *Nebraska History,* Fall, 1969, pp. 293-308.

Forsyth, George A., *Thrilling Days in Army Life,* Harper & Brothers, New York, New York, 1900.

Grinnell, George Bird, *Pawnee Hero Stories and Folk Tales,* Charles Scribner's Sons, New York, 1893.

Grinnell, George B., *Two Great Scouts,* Arthur Clark Company, 1928, (Reprinted by Bison Books, University of Nebraska Press, Lincoln, Nebraska 1973).

Grinnell, George B., *The Fighting Cheyennes,* University of Oklahoma Press, Norman, Oklahoma, 1956.

Guinn, Jack, 'The Red Man's Last Struggle", *The Denver Post* (Empire Magazine), Ten Part Series, 1966.

Hafen, Leroy R., and Ann Hafen, *Our State: Colorado,* The Old West Publishing Company, Denver, Colorado 1966.

Hall, J. N., "Colorado's Early Indian Troubles as I View Them", *The Colorado Magazine,* Vol. XV, No. 4, 1938.

Hamil, Harold, *Colorado Without Mountains,* The Lowell Press, Kansas City, Missouri, 1976.

Hassrick, Royal B., *The Sioux,* University of Oklahoma Press, Norman, Oklahoma, 1964.

Hassrick, Royal B., *The American West,* Octopus Books Ltd., London, 1975.

Hoig, Stan, *The Sand Creek Massacre,* University of Oklahoma Press, Norman, Oklahoma, 1961.

Holmes, Louis A., *Fort McPherson, Nebraska,* Johnson Publishing Co., Lincoln, Nebraska, 1958.

Hyde, George E., *Indians of the High Plains,* University of Oklahoma Press, Norman, Oklahoma, 1959.

Hyde, George E., *Red Cloud's Folk,* University of Oklahoma Press, Norman, Oklahoma, 1937.

Hyde, George, *The Pawnee Indians,* University of Oklahoma Press, Norman, Oklahoma, 1973.

Hyde, George E., *Life of George Bent,* University of Oklahoma Press, Norman, Oklahoma, 1968.

Jones, Douglas, *The Treaty of Medicine Lodge,* University of Oklahoma Press, Norman, 1966.

King, Major General Charles, "Summit Springs", *The Denver Post,* March, 1914.

King, James T., *War Eagle, Life of General Eugene Carr,* University of Nebraska Press, Lincoln, Nebraska, 1963.

King, James T., "The Republican River Expedition", *Nebraska History,* Vol. 41, Nos. 3 and 4, 1960.

Kloberdanz, Timothy, *High as the Eagle Flies,* Private Publication, 1969.

Kloberdanz, Timothy, *The Tragedy at Summit Springs,* Private Publication, 1970.

Krakel, Dean F., *South Platte Country,* Powder River Publishers, Laramie, Wyoming, 1954.

Liberty, Margot and John Stands in Timber, *Cheyenne Memories,* University of Nebraska Press, Lincoln, Nebraska, 1972.

Martin, CY, *The Saga of the Buffalo,* Hart Publishing Company, Inc., New York, New York, 1973.

Mattes, Merrill J., *The Great Platte River Road,* Nebraska State Historical Society, Lincoln, Nebraska, 1969.

McCaffree, Robert H., "The Summit Springs Story", *Sterling Journal Advocate,* July, 1969.

Meredith, Grace E., *Girl Captives of the Cheyennes,* Gem Publishing Company, Lost Angeles, California, 1927.

Moody, Ralph, *Stagecoach West,* Thomas Y. Crowell Company, New York, New York, 1967.

Morison, Samuel E., *The Oxford History of the American People,* Oxford University Press, New York, New York, 1965.

Muilenburg, Grace, and Ada Swineford, *The Land of the Post Rock,* The University Press of Kansas, Lawrence, 1975.

Murdock, C. M., "The Indian Trouble on the Frontier -- Scenes and Difficulties, as taken from a Diary Kept", *The Western Observer,* July, 1869.

Nichols, Alice, *Bleeding Kansas,* Oxford University Press, New York, 1954.

Nye, Wilbur S., *Bad Medicine and Good (Tales of the Kiowas),* University of Oklahoma Press, Norman, Oklahoma, 1962.

Nye, Wilbur S., *Plains Indian Raiders,* University of Oklahoma Press, Norman, Oklahoma, 1968.

Parkman, Francis Jr., *The California and Oregon Trail,* M. A. Donohue & Company, Chicago, Illinois, 1904.

Peate, J. J., "Historical Sketches", *Lincoln Sentinel-Republican,* September 1, 1932.

Price, George F., *Across the Continent with the Fifth Cavalry,* D. Van Nostrand Company, New York, New York, 1883, (Reprinted by Antiquarian Press, Ltd., New York, New York, 1959.)

Reckmeyer, Clarence, "The Battle of Summit Springs", *The Colorado Magazine,* Vol. VI, No. 6, 1929.

Rennert, Jack, *100 Posters of Buffalo Bill's Wild West,* Darien House, New York, New York, 1976.

Rister, Carl C., *Border Captives,* University of Oklahoma Press, Norman, Oklahoma, 1940.

Rister, Carl C., *Border Command, General Phil Sheridan in the West,* University of Oklahoma Press, Norman, Oklahoma, 1944.

Roenigk, Adolph, *Pioneer History of Kansas,* Lincoln County Publication, Kansas, 1933.

Rolfson, Charles M., "Story of Tall Bull", *Sterling Advocate,* January, 1934.

Russell, Don, *The Lives and Legends of Buffalo Bill,* University of Oklahoma Press, Norman, Oklahoma, 1960.

Sandoz, Mari, *Cheyenne Autumn,* McGraw-Hill, New York, New York, 1953.

Silvergerg, Robert, *Home of the Red Man,* Washington Square Press, New York, New York, 1971.

Smith, Washington, "Historical Sketch of the Early Settlement and Organization of Lincoln County", *Lincoln Sentinel-Republican,* April 8, 1926.

Sorrenson, Alfred, "Quarter of the Century on the Frontier or the Adventures of Frank North", (Chapter 12), Unpublished manuscript, Nebraska State Historical Society Archives.

Sparks, Ray G., *Reckoning At Summit Springs,* Lowell Press, Kansas City, Missouri.

Sparks, Ray G., "Tall Bull's Captives", *The Trail Guide,* Vol. VI, No. 1, 1962.

Sprague, Marshall, "Where Bill Cody Killed Tall Bull", *The New York Times,* July 6, 1969.

Stone, Wilbur, *History of Colorado,* Volume I., Chicago, Illinois, 1918.

Stone, Irving, *Men to Match My Mountains,* Doubleday and Company, Inc., Garden City, New York, 1956.

Sumner, Captain Sam, "Report on Summit Springs Battle", *Army and Navy Journal,* Vol. VI, August, 1869.

Taylor, Colin, *The Warriors of the Plains,* The Hamlyn Publishing Group, Ltd., London, 1975.

Thomas, Alfred B., *After Coronado,* University of Oklahoma Press, Norman, Oklahoma, 1935.

Thrapp, Dan L., *The Conquest of Apacheria,* University of Oklahoma Press, Norman, Oklahoma, 1970.

Trenholm, Virginia Cole, *The Arapahoes, Our People,* University of Oklahoma Press, Norman, Oklahoma, 1970.

Tunison, Edgar D., "The Summit Springs Battle", *Sterling Journal Advocate,* August, 1969.

Ubbelohde, Carl, and Maxine Benson, and Duane A. Smith, *A Colorado History,* Pruett Publishing Company, Boulder, Colorado, 1972.

Vestal, S., *Warpath and Council Fire,* Random House, New York, New York, 1948.

Walker, Lester, "Battle of Summit Springs", *North Platte Telegraph,* March, 1967.

Ware, Captain Eugene F., *The Indian War of 1864,* Crane and Company, 1911, Copyright 1960 by Clyde C. Walton, (Reprinted by Bison Books, University of Nebraska Press, Lincoln, Nebraska, 1963).

Watson, E. S., "Summit Springs Battle", *Barber County Index,* September 23, 1937.

Watson, John, "Massacres Once Terrorized Lincoln County", *Wichita Evening Eagle,* April 16, 1953.

Weingardt, Janice, "Early Days of Sterling, Colorado", Unpublished Manuscript, Denver, Colorado.

Wellman, Paul I., "How the Fifth Cavalry Hunted Down and Slew Tall Bull, Leader of the Dog Soldiers", *Wichita Eagle,* December 16, 1930.

Wells, Dale, *The Logan County Ledger,* Logan County Historical Society, Colorado, 1976.

Westermeier, Clifford P., *Colorado's First Portrait,* University of New Mexico Press, Albuquerque, New Mexico, 1970.

Wetmore, Helen Cody, *Last of the Great Scouts,* Duluth Press Publishing Co., 1899, (Reprinted by Bison Book Co., University of Nebraska Press, Lincoln, Nebraska, 1965.)

White, Lonnie J., "Indian Raids on the Kansas Frontier, 1869", *The Kansas Historical Quarterly,* Vol. 38, No. 4, 1972.

Whiteford, Andrew Hunter, *North American Indian Arts,* Golden Press, New York, (Western Publishing Company, Inc.), 1970.

Wieler, Hank, *Old Julesburg,* Private Publication, 1972.

Wynkoop, Edward W., *Colorado History,* Unpublished Manuscript at Colorado State Historical Society.

Yost, Nellie Snyder, *The Call of the Range,* Nebraska Stock Growers Association, 1953.

Zeigler, Eli, "Story of an Indian Raid", *Lincoln Sentinel,* October 18, 1909.

__________, Official Record: Republican River Expedition, 1869, National Archives, Washington, D.C.

__________, Journal: The March of the Republican River Expedition, 1869, National Archives, Washington, D.C.

__________, Official Post Records: Fort Sedgwick, Colorado, 1869, National Archives, Washington, D.C.

__________, Official Post Records: Fort McPherson, Nebraska, 1869, National Archives, Washington, D.C.

__________, "Record of Engagements with Hostile Indians, 1869-1882," Lt. General P. H. Sheridan, Commanding, (Compiled from Official Records, Military Division of the Missouri) Chicago, Illinois, 1882.